Luck Be a Lady Pirate

Sass and Steam
Book 5

CATHERINE STEIN

ISBN: 978-1-949862-43-0

Book cover and interior design by E. McAuley: *emcauley.com*

For notes on content please visit
catsteinbooks.com/content-notes

To anyone who has ever wanted to be a pirate.
May you find your crew.

1

Savannah, Georgia
September 24, 1906

THIS WAS NOT THE FIRST TIME Catalina Navarro had found a
pirate at her front door. Ordinarily, it happened on a schedule,
when the visiting pirate had booked an appointment for her
services. Pirates, Lina knew, were people like any other. Out
of all her clients, they were often the most punctual and
respectful. More women were finding careers outside the home
these days, but Lina remained an oddity in the eyes of society.
Pirates didn't care, as long as she did her job.

Today's pirate had no appointment.

In fact, today's pirate had interrupted an important
telephone call with a prominent psychologist. Lina's insightful
comments on the female mind and its complexity—neither
more nor less inscrutable than the male—had been cut short
by the pirate's inconsiderate pounding. Now Dr. Goodfellow
would go on believing women's brains could be damaged by
too much education and high thinking.

Catalina glared at the woman standing outside her door.
Of course it was her. Who else would barge into her life at

so inopportune a moment but this chaotic vixen, with her avaricious gaze and her haughty manners?

"Miss Redbeard." Lina gave no nod or other gesture of welcome. "Why are you here?"

"Where is the biomechanologist?" the pirate demanded. Her pale blue eyes blazed, like ice cold enough to burn your skin. They were irritatingly beautiful, those eyes.

All of her was irritatingly beautiful, in fact, and it had nothing to do with typical cliches such as porcelain skin or flaxen hair. No, it was in the shape of her mouth—the way her lips could form an obnoxious smirk one moment and the sweetest of smiles the next. It was the uninhibited energy in her movements, as if a boisterous child wore the body of a grown woman. It was a face both so artless and so guarded Lina forgot to breathe every time she beheld it.

"Where has she gone?" Redbeard snapped. "Answer me!"

Lina blinked. Blast it all, she'd been caught staring. Usually she had better control over herself than this. It must have been the stress of the unexpected interruption.

"You are looking for Dr. Taylor?" Lina guessed.

"Oui. Dr. Nora. She repaired her house but no longer lives there. Where is she? Did she marry her giant grumpy man?" The pirate bounced on the balls of her feet. Her hands were clenched like she wanted to fight someone.

"As a matter of fact, she did," Catalina replied coolly. "I can give you her telephone—"

"No. An address. Now."

And that was exactly the problem with the beautiful Miss Redbeard. She didn't listen. She simply threw herself into situations and hoped they worked out. Under special circumstances, such recklessness was understandable. It had served Nora well when Redbeard had assisted in a shockingly dangerous infiltration of a villain's experimental airship. As Lina understood, however, the pirate now on her doorstep lived that way all the time.

She shuddered.

"Nora is in St. Louis," Lina began, only to be interrupted once more.

"You know where? Her address? Her house?" The pirate tapped her foot impatiently.

"Yes." Lina drew the word out, debating whether it ought to be the last thing she said in this increasingly bothersome conversation.

"Good. Brigid! Esme!"

A pair of women in not-quite-matching blue uniforms sprang from nowhere to flank Redbeard. Each of them held a knife. Had they been lurking in the bushes this entire time? Waiting to intimidate her, probably.

Well, little did they know, but Catalina carried a knife of her own. She wasn't an easy woman to intimidate. And she certainly wasn't rewarding this rudeness with Nora's address. Especially since Nora would probably smile at everyone and invite them all in for tea. Knives didn't deserve tea.

"Bring her along," the pirate captain commanded. "We will learn what we need when we are in the air."

The words made no sense until hands clamped down on both of Lina's arms. Brigid and Esme hauled her down the stairs and into the street.

"This way," said the one Lina thought was Esme. Her tone was distressingly pleasant from someone brandishing a knife and digging her nails into Lina's arm.

"Is not far." Brigid's grip was like a manacle.

"Damn you, you can't kidnap me!" Lina shouted. Hopefully her neighbors would hear.

Hopefully her neighbors would hear and do something to help instead of phoning one another to gossip about it.

"Your information is necessary," Redbeard said, sounding perfectly reasonable. She probably believed she *was* reasonable. She closed Lina's door—perhaps the only actually reasonable thing she'd done today—and jogged to catch up with Lina and her captors.

Three against one. It was hopeless. Lina couldn't even slow them down by dragging her feet. The pirate women were too strong.

"It is a matter of life and death," Redbeard explained as the group hurried down the street. "Even the remaining journey may be too long. We must fly now, as quickly as possible."

Lina stumbled along, her arms beginning to ache where the pirates held her. "You can't barge up to someone's door and drag them away with you!"

"I can." Redbeard tossed her long blond curls. "I'm sorry. I will return you when I can. Now, we *must* fly." Her voice nearly cracked on the last syllable.

Lina sucked in a sharp breath. The pirate captain was distraught beneath her domineering behavior. Lina had suspected from their first, brief meeting that sadness lingered in the woman's heart, but this was something more immediate. She was afraid.

Does she fear for herself? For someone else? What trauma lies in her past? What troubles grieve her heart now, driving her to this?

"Oh, hell," Lina muttered.

Now she'd done it. She'd started analyzing the exasperating beauty. Next she'd start sympathizing. Then she'd start longing. To help. To hold. To comfort. Not a good way to squelch the lust she already felt every time their eyes met.

"You understand?" the pirate asked. "You won't give me trouble?"

"Trouble," Lina huffed, shaking her head.

As if *she* could be the trouble. Trouble was a scrawny, golden-haired Frenchwoman with a perfect face and secret pain. Trouble was what Catalina Navarro wanted least.

And maybe also most.

2

YVETTE HAD NO TIME TO MAKE NICE. Every second brought Olga closer to death, and as the captain, Yvette couldn't allow that. Not if there was any possible way to save her.

She barked orders to her crew, waiting at their stations in the airship above. The moment Yvette and the others stepped onto the cargo lift, La Liberté began to rise into the air.

Miss Navarro gave a cry of alarm, though she quickly smothered it beneath another furious glare. She could scowl all she wanted. Yvette had more important concerns at the moment than the hurt feelings of an upper-class lady.

"You may release her." Yvette spoke to Brigid and Esme in French, assuming the American wouldn't understand. "I doubt she is so foolish she would throw herself off the lift."

Even Yvette wouldn't try such a thing from this height. Unless she had a rope she could swing down on. Or a pile of soft materials she could land in. If she timed it right, the canopy sticking out from that nearby building could break her fall.

The sight of Miss Navarro shaking her arms brought Yvette's attention back to her intended task. This was her ship. She was in charge here. No escape plan needed. And no daydreaming allowed. Daydreams got people killed.

Her stomach knotted. They had to save Olga. The crew

needed to know their captain would do all she could to protect them.

The voices pounded in her head.

"Little Yvette made another mistake."

"Don't give her any important jobs."

"Why is she even a Sister?"

"Spoiled princess with her head in the clouds."

Yvette bit her lower lip. That would not be her. Not anymore. Never again.

The moment the lift settled into place, Yvette vaulted over the rail onto the deck. Behind her, the gate clanked open. Miss Navarro, no doubt, using the door in proper fashion. Proper and Yvette had never mixed well.

"How is she?" Yvette, still speaking French, turned to the nearest crewwoman, a seventeen-year-old Swiss girl in an ill-fitting uniform and sloppy pigtails.

The teenager—one of two sisters rescued during the operation in which Olga had sustained her injuries—gave a tiny shrug of her shoulders. "No change. Clara is watching her. It's my turn to rest."

Ah. This twin was Chantal, then. "Go rest," Yvette told the girl. "You need strength. I've brought help."

The girl shrugged again and wandered off, looking painfully like Yvette's past self. Lost. Alone.

I will do this. I will save Olga. Clara and Chantal will have the chance to learn and be true crew members.

"Esme, have my cabin prepared for Mademoiselle Navarro."

Yvette couldn't help but glance at the woman when she spoke her name. Tall. Proud. Very professional in her tidy white shirt and perfectly pressed skirt. A pair of black suspenders curved around her breasts, highlighting them as neatly as a low-cut gown would have. A deliberate attempt to be alluring in her modest garb? Or merely an accident of fashion?

Yvette knew little about Miss Navarro except that she was a friend of Nora's and an occasional collaborator. Not a medical doctor, but some sort of lady scientist. Perhaps she could be of use to Olga during the journey.

"Then see that she is escorted to the sickbay to give any help she can."

Esme nodded. "Aye, Captain."

"I'm going to the helm."

Yvette sprinted up to the bridge and slipped into the pilot's position, giving a nod of thanks to Angelique for taking a shift.

"De rien," the soft-spoken Black woman murmured. She hurried below, probably to check on Olga.

I will save her.

Yvette's muscles began to uncramp as she positioned them comfortably on the wheel. This was where she belonged. From here, she could see the entire ship and the sky in front of them. Her hands would be constantly busy, tweaking the steering or adjusting the gauges. Her crew would manage all the other parts of the ship and Yvette could fly free.

She pushed La Liberté to top speed, a feat none of the other women would have dared. But the air was Yvette's home. Flying was the one task where the noises in her brain always quieted and she could simply be. Exist.

The sky had fallen completely dark by the time her first mate came to take a shift. Yvette stepped aside, a sudden exhaustion overtaking her as she slipped out of her focus. How long had it been since she'd taken the helm? How long had it been since she'd slept?

Zahra took the wheel and Yvette mumbled a word of thanks. A few hours' rest. That's all she needed, and then she'd be back, pushing her ship harder, showing her crew she wasn't a tag-along child. Or, worse, her father.

Yvette stumbled across the deck, down the stairs, and through the narrow corridor to her cabin. Her bed awaited her, soft and warm. A half-night's sleep couldn't hurt. The crew wouldn't let her down.

She pulled open the door, revealing an uninterrupted

swath of darkness. Strange. She usually left the bedside light on so she could find her way around. Blasted bulbs, always burning out.

Yvette groped for the switch by the door, flicking it to illuminate the room with the overhead electric light. A woman's clothes lay folded on her reading chair, and the woman they belonged to lay in Yvette's bed.

Merde.

She'd forgotten about putting Miss Navarro here. There wasn't any place else appropriate for a guest, so the decision had made sense, but at the time Yvette had been preoccupied with Olga and the need to take the helm. Even now, she barely remembered giving the order.

"Wha—?" Miss Navarro murmured sleepily. Her glossy black hair spilled across the crisp white of the freshly laundered pillow. She stretched one long, bare arm above her head and the quilt covering her slid down to expose her neck and shoulder.

Heat washed over Yvette's entire body. There was a naked woman sleeping in *her* bed. How embarrassing. How thrillingly wicked.

The appropriately piratical thing to do would be to growl, "Move over, wench!" and slide into the bed next to her. But that was too wicked, even for Yvette. She'd never been a good pirate, no matter how she tried.

She grabbed one of the pillows off the bed and pulled the extra quilt from the storage trunk beside it.

"What are you… doing here?" Miss Navarro mumbled, her voice raspy.

Yvette quickly shut off the light and curled up on the floor. "It's my room," she retorted. "Be grateful I'm sharing it."

Rest. She needed rest. Then she could get back to work. Soon enough, she'd be rid of the annoying Miss Navarro and back in her own bed, content with the knowledge that she'd protected her crew and done something right.

For once.

3

$\mathcal{T}$HE PIRATE WAS GONE. Catalina might have thought she'd been nothing more than a dream, except for the quilt and pillow on the floor. Well, and the certainty that if she'd been a dream, she would have climbed into bed for some lusty fun.

"Oh, for heaven's sake, Lina," she muttered to herself.

Captain Redbeard was a thief, a kidnapper, and a disruption to Catalina's orderly life. Not an object of girlish fantasies. Lina knew well the havoc wreaked by chasing such fantasies, and she had no intention of repeating her youthful mistake. A romp with a pirate was out of the question, no matter how much fun it might be.

A knock sounded on the door, and Lina adjusted the quilt to cover herself. "Come in."

A woman entered and set a bundle of clothing atop the chest at the foot of the bed.

Twinkling dark-brown eyes met Lina's. "Good morning," the woman said, in accented English. "My name is Kaina, and I am the purser here on La Liberté."

Her uniform consisted of a white underskirt and top with military-style buttons and trim down the center. These were covered with a long-sleeved, royal blue over-dress, worn like a jacket and buckled at the waist with an intricate silver belt.

Swirls of organic embroidery decorated the hem. A matching blue scarf wrapped around her head and neck.

Lina's gaze shifted to the pile of clothing. All blue and white, with silver accents. The stack of items matched what Kaina wore, but none of it appeared to be exactly the same. Much like what she'd seen the other women wearing.

"You all wear uniforms, but each one is tailored to your personal heritage and preferences," Lina guessed.

Kaina grinned. "We do. The captain wants the crew to be a team, but not to take away our individuality. I've brought a number of items that we were able to spare. You may pick and choose from them as you like. The captain wanted you to have clean clothing for the duration of your stay with us."

Duration of her stay? Just how long did they intend to keep her here? St. Louis was a single day's flight.

"Thank you, Kaina." Lina gave the purser a smile. The crew here were not enemies. It was their captain who was responsible. And Lina intended to give Redbeard a thorough tongue-lashing the moment she was able.

"You're welcome," Kaina replied. "If you need anything else, please ask for me, as I'm in charge of all the equipment, supplies, and logistics onboard. I'll leave you to dress now." She nodded and departed.

Lina tossed aside the coverlet and sorted through the pile of uniform pieces, laying them out by type: skirts, trousers, shirts, jackets. The styles and sizes were varied, but enough of them would fit to offer her a bit of choice.

She settled on a pair of blue trousers and a loose white top she might have termed a "pirate shirt" even if it hadn't literally belonged to a pirate. The trousers were a size too large, so she donned her suspenders to prevent them from sagging. With the pirate shirt tucked in, her reflection in the small mirror looked reasonably presentable.

After twisting her hair up into the primmest knot she

could manage, Lina left the cabin and stalked up the stairs to confront her captor.

Dawn colored the sky a soft pink, dotted by fluffy white clouds. Did that mean a storm was coming? Or was a red morning a sign of fair weather? She could never remember.

A gust of wind whipped straight through Lina's shirt, and she shivered. Blast. She ought to have put on another layer. She began to turn back, when her gaze snagged on Redbeard. The pirate captain stared down from her place at the helm, directly at Lina. The wind tossed her unbound curls and made her long, brown coat billow out around her.

A warrior goddess.

Lina scowled at the ridiculous thought. Redbeard was a woman like any other, and Lina would not be intimidated.

Ignoring the bite of the wind, she marched across the deck and up to the bridge, planting herself only a few feet from the wheel.

"We will be in St. Louis in one hour," the captain stated. "I will send someone to fetch you when we need your directions. Go below and help Olga."

Lina saw no reason to comply with anything Redbeard demanded. Especially if she couldn't even be bothered to ask nicely.

"I can't help her. I saw her last night, and she was barely conscious. There was nothing I could do. I'm not a doctor, I'm a psychological therapist."

"I don't know what that is."

No one knew what it was. Sometimes Lina thought she spent more time explaining her profession than practicing it.

She took a deep breath, then recited the words she had perfected over the years. "I study the human brain and behavior. These psychological studies allow me to help others suffering from mental and emotional issues. My goal is for my clients to leave my services with a better understanding of themselves and a greater ability to face their troubles."

"Interesting," Redbeard murmured, her tone suggesting the opposite.

Lina put her hands on her hips. "This is exactly the problem with you. You're rude. You go about doing whatever you want without concern for the feelings of others. Did you expect me to *like* being kidnapped? To simply fall into place and start obeying your orders? Is that how you got yourself a crew? I suppose I ought to have expected it of a pirate, but after you helped Nora, I thought you were different. That maybe you weren't entirely—"

Catalina's words ground to a halt. The pirate captain had both hands on the wheel, her back straight and her eyes looking everywhere but at Lina.

"Are you even listening to me?"

Redbeard didn't respond. The airship rocked and her expression tightened.

Lina sighed. "Look, I don't like to interrupt you while you're driving, but otherwise you'll walk away, and you need to hear this. You owe me an apology. If you'd been more polite, I could have given you the address and you could have—"

The airship swayed again, abruptly enough that Lina had to stagger to keep her balance.

"Rough air on the descent!" Redbeard shouted. "Find your places and hold tight!" She spared a tiny glance in Lina's direction. "Sit down."

"Would it hurt you to say please? Consider it for a moment. How would you feel— Oof!" Lina fell against the control panel as the ship bounced even harder than before. "Right."

She unhooked her shirt from where it had caught on some spinning indicator, then sat. Seated on the deck, she was not only more stable, but also shielded from the wind.

"C-c-captain?" A frightened voice called out.

Lina pushed up on her knees, craning her neck to see over the controls without standing. One of the twin girls that had been watching over the injured woman came rushing up to the helm, her face white and her arms hugged to her chest.

"I d-don't have a task," the young woman babbled. "Chantal is on watch. I don't know what to do. Where should I go? Are we in d-danger?"

"Sit," Redbeard commanded, pointing to the deck where Lina sat.

The girl obeyed, falling clumsily to her bottom as the air currents tossed the ship about.

"Miss Navarro helps troubled people," the captain continued. "She will help you, Clara."

Lina blinked. So she *had* been listening. At least somewhat.

"Clara." Lina extended a hand. "My name is Catalina. Lina to my friends. It's a pleasure to meet you."

The teenager placed her hand in Lina's. "Thank you. I'm Clara Favre. N-new pirate." Despite the tremor, she said the word "pirate" as if it were a badge of honor.

"First time in rough air?"

Clara gave a half-laugh. "First time for everything outside of school. We'd been there so long. There's... so much I don't know."

"And there always will be. I learn new things often, and I'm almost twice your age. It's nothing to be ashamed of."

"Thank you." Clara's grip tightened on Lina's hand as the ship pitched. "Are you scared, too?"

"No." Lina looked up at Redbeard. "Look at the captain. She is focused, but not afraid. Her skills will keep us safe."

Clara nodded.

"Tell me something about yourself," Lina suggested. A distraction would do the girl good. "About your school. Or how you came to be a new pirate."

"Oh, the school had problems. Dissension in the ranks, you could call it. Something happened early this year, and suddenly there was arguing and fighting where there never had been before. Some of our projects and classes ended abruptly.

Some teachers vanished without a word. No one would tell the students what the trouble was, as if we were too naive to notice."

"That does sound troubling."

Clara nodded vigorously. "One of my teachers arranged an educational holiday for the students nearing graduation, like me and Chantal. We were to spend a month traveling. We were so excited, and pleased to get away from the strange whispers and squabbling. We flew to Paris. But something went wrong and a group of men attacked us."

She shuddered and fell suddenly silent. There was more to this story, Lina knew, but she wouldn't press the girl. Earning her trust was the first and most important step in the process.

"The pirates rescued us," Clara finished. "That's why I want to be one of them. I want to be strong and brave."

Lina gave her hand a squeeze. "I think you already are. And do you feel that? The bouncing has stopped. I told you the captain had things under control."

Lina glanced up again, and this time Redbeard looked back. Looked right into Lina's eyes, unblinking. The wind still toyed with the pirate's blond hair, fanning it out behind her when she cocked her head to one side. Her ice-blue eyes gleamed with speculation.

All the breath whooshed out of Lina's lungs. The captain was interested in her. Lina had dallied with enough ladies to recognize subtle signs of attraction. Redbeard's lips had parted slightly, and her pupils had widened.

No assumptions. But there was potential in that penetrating gaze. Good God, how she longed for just a little kiss from those pouty lips.

"I think I like you, Catalina Navarro." The pirate's mouth curved into a smirk. "When you're not being prissy."

Prissy? The word shook Lina from her lust-fueled haze. She sprang to her feet.

"Well, Miss Redbeard, I'm afraid I still don't like you

at all." She turned away. "I'll go downstairs and see how the patient is faring. Clara, would you like to join me?"

Lina started off, trying to maintain as casual and un-prissy a manner as possible.

"You may call me Yvette," the captain shouted after her.

4

LINA USED HER LONGER STRIDE to cut in front of Yvette before she could start pounding on Nora's door. She rang the bell like a respectable person and waited.

Behind her, muttered French words mingled with the sounds of rustling cloth. Yvette, fidgeting again. It was her nature, Lina suspected, not merely eagerness to get her injured employee to a doctor.

The door to Nora's surgery swung open.

"Lina!" A joyous smile lit Nora's face, and she bounced in place, tossing her short blond hair. "You didn't tell me you were coming!" A wrinkle of confusion appeared in her brow as she took in the scene behind Lina. "And you brought pirates?"

Lina had no chance to answer. The two strongest pirates, Esme and Zahra, elbowed past her, carrying Olga through the door.

"Oh, dear!" Nora sprang back to let them in. "Quickly, the door on the left. Place her on the bed. Lina, could you lead the other ladies into the house proper and ring for some refreshments? You know where everything is."

With that, she disappeared into her surgery room and shut the door.

If this had been Nora's old house in Savannah, Lina would

have felt comfortable entertaining. But this house she'd only visited twice, and it had belonged to Mr. Cassidy long before Nora had moved in with him.

Even so, Nora's request stirred a hope of regaining some semblance of order. Catalina ushered the women into the parlor, then arranged for tea, coffee, and snacks. Soon she was seated in a plush armchair, sipping a brisk breakfast tea and nibbling on buttered toast. The other women were also eating and drinking. Quietly. Calmly. Peacefully. As a morning should be.

Warmth flowed through Lina as the tea settled in her stomach. At last, something in the world had righted itself. Now she could think with a clear head. She could look forward to tomorrow, when she would be back at home, on schedule.

Creak!

Lina tried not to look, but her eyes were drawn to the only movement in the room.

Creak!

The rocking chair squeaked again. Yvette—the name suited her so well, Lina could no longer think of her as Redbeard—pushed all the way up on tiptoe to rock the chair back as far as possible before letting it fall forward. She crammed a biscuit into her mouth and repeated the rocking motion. Over and over.

I shouldn't stare. I should not *stare.*

But the rest of the room was so calm, the only noises the trickle of pouring coffee or the *tink* of a teacup settling onto a saucer. It could have been a salon for genteel ladies, if not for Yvette's constant movement.

"These are good." Yvette bounded out of her chair, piled half-a-dozen more biscuits onto her plate, and poured herself more coffee, then proceeded to resume her agitated rocking.

Or perhaps not so agitated. Though she wasn't smiling, her face was unlined, her eyes not downcast. She stared off into the distance, at nothing in particular. If anything, she appeared soothed by the motion of the chair.

Fascinating.

"Das ist ein schönes Haus," Brigid observed.

"Like a palace," Esme agreed. "The bloke the bio-doc married must be a bleedin' toff."

"He discovered luxene." Zahra dipped a corner of her toast into her tea. "It's that green fuel that powers small dragons. Worth a fortune."

And the pirates were off, chattering happily in several languages about the house, the food, what they would do with a million dollars, and so forth. Lina didn't follow the conversation closely. It was background noise. A perfectly typical social event, like she'd attended many times over.

She couldn't tear her attention from Yvette. The pirate captain rocked and stared and rocked and stared, lost in her own world, alone in a room full of people.

She would make a wonderful psychological subject. A study of her thoughts and behaviors might even enhance Lina's understanding of the mind-body connection. Perhaps Yvette's constant motion reflected a mind equally as active. Did impulsive thoughts lead to impulsive movements, or vice versa? If she was amenable, Lina could delve deep into the whats and whys of the pirate captain's actions.

Perhaps after she returned home tomorrow, she could check her schedule and pencil in a session for the next time Yvette flew through Savannah.

Lina had constructed a full mental list of possible questions and activities to explore—was there paper here? She needed to write this down—when Nora swung the door open.

Startled, Lina jostled her tea, splattering the pristine white of her shirt with pale brown droplets. One of the pirates would have to scrub that out, no doubt. Yvette ought to do it, since this entire thing was her fault. She wouldn't, though. She did what she wanted, not what she ought.

"Will she live?" Yvette teetered on the edge of her chair, finally still. Her eyes were wide, her brow creased with worry.

Lina flicked a finger at one of the wet spots on her shirt. Yvette did care for her crew; that was abundantly clear. She wasn't wholly bad.

A criminal with a heart of gold? Honestly, Catalina, you may as well be reading fairy stories.

"She is doing well."

Nora's words brought a collective breath of relief from the pirates.

"She will pull through," Nora went on. "However, her recovery will take several weeks at best. I want to commend you all on the job you did caring for her on your journey here. You stemmed the blood loss and kept the wounds clean, and those things saved her life."

Lina's gaze swept over the assembled pirates. Zahra's cheeks held a coppery sheen and Esme's pale face had turned bright red. Blushing pirates? Who were these women?

Her fingers twitched. This crew held secrets. Fascinating secrets, and she itched to uncover them all.

Nora continued her briefing. "I've found no signs of infection, and there was no damage to any vital organs. While the injuries are not insignificant, I believe much of her weakness stems from a toxic substance in her bloodstream. I'm running tests now to determine the exact nature. I'd like a bit more information about the cause of her wounds. The lacerations look like claw marks, but they would have to be from a monstrously large animal. And no animal I know of has claws tipped in poison."

The pirates looked at one another, lips pinched tight, postures stiff. No one said a word.

"Anything you can tell me might help," Nora prompted.

Lina nodded admiringly. Nora had perfected the combination of professional competence and genuine empathy.

"It was a creature attacking innocent girls," Yvette said at last. "Large with big, wide claws. We destroyed it."

"Mechanical?" Nora asked.

Yvette gave a sharp nod, her jaw clenched.

"And the poison?"

"I do not know." She slid back in her chair. Lina would've bet ten dollars she'd say nothing more.

Lina tapped a single finger against her lips. Innocent girls. Clara and Chantal? Clara had mentioned men attacking them. Men who'd employed a mechanical beast in their assault, perhaps? Her curiosity was so strong her skin tingled.

She forced a calming breath. Merely a physical reaction to a psychological stimulus. One she'd learned to cope with years ago. An inquiring mind was a good thing, but only when tempered with common sense.

This incident was none of her business. She'd played her small role, and that was more than enough.

Creak.

Yvette was rocking again, ice blue eyes looking but not seeing.

Lina forced herself to look away. Tomorrow she was going home.

5

$\mathcal{P}$OISON. The type to cause a long, agonizing death rather than an instantaneous one.

Someone would pay.

Yvette paced the deck in the waning sunlight, reviewing the entire attack in her mind. It was supposed to have been a straightforward commission. Transport half-a-dozen girls to an undisclosed location in exchange for a cache of antiquities worth several thousands. She'd made the arrangements via documents encoded by La Capitaine's unbreakable encryption machine.

Yet someone had known. Those men and their metal beast had been lying in wait. They'd known exactly who to expect.

Yvette and the crew had been lucky to escape with only a single casualty. Kaina's knowledge of hydraulics had disabled the machine and allowed them to flee, but with only two of the girls. Now that Olga was in good hands, it was time to go back for the rest.

Yvette pulled her knife and began to walk through a basic combat drill. Practice. She needed practice. She was Redbeard, and she would not be thwarted. The antiquities were probably long gone, but this was bigger than money. Her enemy would pay.

She completed about half of the knife exercise before her wandering mind caused her to miss a step. Not terrible. Her skills were improving, albeit slowly.

A shift at the helm settled her. Whatever else happened in her life, she could always count on flying to leave her body relaxed and her head clear. Olga was safely in Nora's care. Yvette would sleep better tonight, knowing she'd done the right thing and saved a friend and crewmate.

Sometime near midnight, she bounded down the steps to the lower deck, debating whether to sleep on the floor for one more night or to shove Catalina over and make her share. A nice bed and the enjoyment of irritating a proper lady, but facing her anger and scolding? Or a hard floor but no possibility of anyone bothering her? Hmm.

The room was empty, the door standing wide open.

Prickles slid across Yvette's skin, and her hand fell automatically to the hilt of her knife. A sob echoed through the corridor from somewhere behind her.

Yvette whirled and flew toward the crew bunkrooms. She was a small woman, but long-legged for her size, and it took only seconds to reach the source of the cries. She spun through the doorway and skidded to a halt.

Brigid lay curled on her bunk, weeping into a handkerchief. Beside her sat Miss Navarro, murmuring in a soothing tone and patting her arm.

"They were wrong to say that." Despite the softness of Catalina's voice, her words were firm. "Crying isn't a form of weakness. It's your body's natural response to pain or other strong emotions. You should cry as long and as hard as you need to. It will help relieve both your body and mind."

"But it was… only a dream," Brigid choked out. "I'm… silly."

"You are not," Yvette said vehemently. She knew how painful dreams could be. They all did.

Catalina glanced up at Yvette and smiled. Yvette forgot how

to breathe. The smile made Lina's dark brown eyes gleam like polished mahogany. It brought a glow to her olive complexion. It showed every feature of her face with the perfection of an artistic masterpiece. Who the devil had given her permission to smile like that? She could probably start wars smiling at people that way.

"The captain is absolutely correct," Catalina explained. "Dreams often connect to things that are hurting us or have hurt us in the past. The dream might vanish when you wake, but the pain it leaves is real. Embrace the tears for the good thing they are. Sometimes a single tear is enough to relieve an ache inside you. Sometimes you need to curse and punch pillows."

Brigid sat halfway up, laughing through a sniffle. "Punch pillows? I like that."

She slammed a fist into her pillow. A single feather popped out and drifted across the small room.

"I hate him!" She shouted in German, pounding the pillow again. "I hate how he treated us! I hate how he hurt me and used me and made me feel worthless!" Tears streamed down her face as she beat out her frustrations into the bedding. "I hate how even though he's dead I'm still afraid!"

Yvette's chest tightened. Damn her father to the bowels of hell. Too many women had suffered this same fate, so many not even realizing how thoroughly he was exploiting their skills until they were fully enmeshed in his organization.

Her crew was strong. So strong. But they were also human.

Brigid fluffed the pillow back into shape and straightened up. "I feel better," she said in English. She dabbed away her tears with her handkerchief. "Thank you."

"You're very welcome," Catalina replied. "I'm always pleased when my professional advice can help someone. If the nightmare recurs, you now know a way to recover. You can also try deep breathing exercises, silent meditation or prayer, or simply talking to a friend. Different approaches work for different people, and even at different times. And if you have any more questions or concerns, please seek me out. I am happy to discuss anything, from mundane to vitally important."

"Danke." Brigid extended a hand and Catalina shook it.

"Sleep well, Brigid."

Yvette stepped aside to let Lina pass through the door, then followed her back to her room, excitement bubbling inside. This was exactly what she needed. Maybe Fortune was smiling on her at last.

"You have done it again, Brain Doctor," she applauded.

Catalina paused at the foot of the bed and turned around. "Done what, exactly?"

"Assisted one of my pirates when she was troubled. You're very good. You have a calming way and a professional manner. The women trust you."

Lina's heart-stopping smile returned. "Thank you. It's lovely to be appreciated. Perhaps in the future we might actually get along."

"We will," Yvette declared. "Your skills are valuable. You gave Brigid a way to fight when she felt weak. You told her tears were good, but you also helped her make it true for herself. I am impressed."

"Thank you."

Catalina's lashes lowered. Was she blushing? Remarkable. Yvette would never have suspected coyness or shyness to lurk beneath that oh-so-proper exterior. The woman had depths. And now Yvette would have a chance to discover them.

"This is wonderful. Welcome to the crew. Sleep well. I'll run up and set our course for Paris."

A confused frown replaced Lina's bashful smile. "What?"

"We don't need to stop in Savannah. You're staying with us."

Yvette turned and skipped toward the stairs. Perfect. Everything was working out perfectly. She would rescue the other girls, thwart her enemies, and soon her name would be feared by loathsome men across the globe.

"Wait… What?!"

Nothing would stop her. Not even Catalina's angry, puzzled shouts.

6

THIS WASN'T HAPPENING. It made no sense. She'd misheard.

Lina replayed the conversation in her head. Yvette had been praising her. Thanking her for helping Brigid. And then…

Welcome to the crew?

"Wait!" Lina called again, dashing out the door. She was ninety-percent certain she hadn't agreed to something by mistake. This had to be Yvette being Yvette again.

Curse it, why did this have to happen in the middle of the night when she was tired?

"Stop!" She raced up the stairs. "Yvette, listen to me!"

The pirate froze at the sound of her name.

"What was all that?" Lina demanded. "You can't change our course. You can't kidnap me again."

Yvette turned and put her hands on her hips. "I am not kidnapping you. I am hiring you."

Lina took one furious stride forward, then reconsidered and walked toward Yvette at a more sedate pace.

"Certain conventions are to be expected when hiring someone. One, you tell them what the job is. Two, you *ask* if they want to do it. Three, you settle on a fair arrangement, such as amount of work, hours of work, payment, and so forth."

Yvette waved a hand. "You know what the job is, and the

money will be good. Ask any of the crew. They are satisfied with our earnings."

"And the asking?" Lina took one more step forward, looming over the shorter woman. "The most important part?"

Yvette tilted her chin up defiantly and hot desire flooded through Lina's body. She clenched her fists. Why was this insolent little thief so maddeningly tempting? It was as if she were daring Lina to kiss her.

"Asking was unnecessary," Yvette declared, sounding as if she genuinely believed it. "You are coming with us. In Savannah you have only boring old men and lonely rich ladies. Here you have pirates. Travel. Adventure. And women you can help. You like helping them. It shows on your face."

Tempting. Tempting. God, so tempting. A steady stream of clients who genuinely needed her. The camaraderie of a group of interesting and diverse women. A captain with secrets and a perfect mouth.

"I don't like adventure," Lina argued, trying to quash the childish glee bubbling in the back of her mind.

This is not a fairytale. She is not a damsel. You are not her knight.

Yvette's blond brows lifted. "Don't be silly. Everyone likes adventure. Who would want a boring life?"

"Many people do. I do."

Do you, though? Have you truly been content a single day since Nora left?

The clients Nora had sent her had always been the most interesting. The rest were retired smugglers who were more lonely than troubled and ladies with little to do but spread society gossip. A once-a-week social club would help them as much as Lina could.

"You do not like boring," Yvette insisted. "You like my ship. You like my crew. You like us because we are the same as you. We are different than the world you come from."

The words were so true Lina almost staggered. Back

home, she'd never fit in. Her family supported her, yet they'd considered her an oddity since she was a girl. And her dearest childhood friend—a true kindred spirit, she'd once believed—had spurned her in favor of a path she still couldn't comprehend. Years of study at a feminist university and connections with other women of sapphic inclinations had proven she wasn't alone, but a true sense of community eluded her.

Lina doubted she'd find it in a pirate crew, but an opportunity for travel would provide a wider perspective. Maybe it could lead her to a place she did belong.

She corrected her posture and smoothed down a wrinkle in her shirt. Catalina Navarro did not react impulsively. She had years of practice channeling her natural curiosity and desire for new experiences into her scientific studies.

"You are different," she agreed. "And interesting. But I will not rush headlong into lawlessness merely for the company of interesting women."

"Merely?" Yvette turned up her nose. "We are not mere anything. We are pirates and ladies. We defy the rules and claim our freedom. We fly and fight and do things that women are told not to do. You do too, or you would not be a scientist who is a friend of Dr. Nora."

"That is true." Lina could hardly claim to have followed the path society suggested for her. "Nevertheless..."

"And when I am infamous?" Yvette interrupted. "I am the dread pirate Rebeard. When women beg to join my crew and men tremble in fear at my name, do you want to read it in a newspaper? Or do you want to have lived the story yourself?" She smiled coquettishly. "Come, Catalina. Come and see for yourself."

Lina's pulse began to race.

"How much is the pay? I need a number."

The words were out of her mouth before her brain thought through the implications. Dammit! She'd given in to Yvette's demands. God, she hoped this wasn't simply an illogical reaction to feeling trapped on the ship. The last time she'd attempted something this outlandish she'd made an utter ass of herself and lost Emily's friendship all at once.

The captain's blue eyes sparkled in the lantern-light. "Take your usual weekly earnings and add twenty percent to start."

"That's fair." More than fair, considering her room and board would also be included. She could rent out her house in Savannah and earn even more while she was out of town. A few months on the ship would give her quite a nice pile of savings. Maybe this idea wasn't so outlandish after all.

"Of course it's fair. If I am to be the best pirate, I must have the best crew. Therefore, they must deserve the best pay."

Lina ticked off the potential benefits on a mental checklist. A break from her currently solitary life. Excellent pay. Unique companions. Travel. Opportunities for scientific study. Flirtations with a beautiful woman.

No, scratch that last one. If she was going to do this, she would do it in a wholly sensible way that had nothing to do with fantasies of any nature.

"Very well," she said with long-practiced calm. "I accept."

Yvette bounced and flashed her impish smile. "See? I knew you would. I'm going to change our course now."

She turned to walk away, but Lina grabbed her arm to stop her. "No, wait."

Yvette's entire body went rigid. A moment later she wrenched herself from Lina's grasp.

Lina jogged after her, taking care not to touch her again. "I'm sorry. I didn't mean to startle you." It had been much more than simple startlement, but she wouldn't press Yvette about it. "I only wanted to say that I need to return to Savannah. I have books and clothes and personal items I need."

Yvette turned slowly. "I see. And you cannot do without these things?"

"I would much prefer clothes that fit, I need my health and grooming items, and my books are absolutely necessary if I am to do my job to the best of my ability. I can't hold everything in my brain at once, so I keep references."

Yvette crossed her arms and tapped her foot. "I don't like it."

"Do you really think I would agree to your employment offer and then run off the moment we land in Savannah?"

The captain said nothing. The toe of her boot drummed a steady rhythm against the deck.

Damnation.

That was it. That was the reason for her imperious behavior. Yvette didn't trust.

She hadn't trusted Lina to reveal Nora's address. She didn't trust any doctor but Nora with Olga's care—or to keep quiet about it, presumably. Now she didn't trust Lina to truly accept the offered position.

"I accepted your proposal," Lina said, slipping into her soothing psychological therapist voice. "I won't go back on my word."

"Others have said that to me before," Yvette challenged.

"I'm sure they have. I, however, am sincere."

Lina's course seemed crystal clear now. She'd done this before. Trust took time to build. It couldn't be stated, only demonstrated. Yvette apparently had some betrayal in her past. Convincing her would require a consistent effort.

"Allow me to stop in Savannah and collect my belongings," Lina requested. "When I return promptly, prepared to step into the role of ship's mental health advisor, you will know I am loyal to the crew. Consider it my first mission as a pirate."

Yvette twisted a strand of hair around one finger, once again staring off into the distance. "You are smart. You can bargain. You are brave. A little soft, but we can make you tough. I think you can be a pirate."

Soft? Lina was *not* soft.

"I know how to use a knife," she snapped.

"Good. Then you will need less training." Yvette stopped

fidgeting and turned her gaze back to Lina. "I will take you to Savannah. You will gather whatever things you desire. In return for this favor, you will also bring something nice for the crew. Scented soaps or bath oils, perhaps. We are modern, sophisticated pirates. We like to be clean and pretty."

"I would be happy to procure something of that nature for all the women," Lina agreed. "Now, I think I should turn in so I will be rested when we arrive. Good night." She nodded to Yvette and headed for the stairs.

There. She'd won.

7

YVETTE EYED THE ARRAY of perfume bottles tucked into the substantial box of health and beauty supplies Catalina had brought onboard. Fine French perfumes, all of them. Not a single cheap imitation. The glorious assortment only increased the giddiness that had washed over her when Lina had returned to the ship, good to her word.

Yvette closed a greedy hand over a pyramid-shaped green bottle.

Yes.

Coeur Mortelle. Her signature scent. She dabbed a small amount on her neck and down between her breasts. The sandalwood and cedar base notes filled her nostrils, adding a depth and earthiness to the orange blossom and bergamot anchoring the top and middle notes.

Perfection.

She'd stolen a bottle as an adolescent, using it judiciously over the course of several years. Only now could she afford to obtain it legally—assuming one considered payment with money earned through theft and smuggling to be a legal transaction.

"I'll have these moved to the bathing chamber," Kaina said. "Now we won't need to replenish our supplies when we reach Paris. I've also seen to the refilling of the cisterns. We will have plenty of water for the voyage, both for the boilers and for washing and cooking."

"Merci." Yvette tucked the perfume into a small pocket inside her coat. "Have you found room for all Miss Navarro's things?"

"We're converting the forward storeroom in the cargo hold to her office. It has windows, plus the shelves she needs. We've made a temporary bunk, but will need to purchase a permanent one and a desk when we reach Paris."

"Excellent. I'll prepare the ship for takeoff."

Yvette bounded up into the sunshine. Today was glorious. A bright blue sky stretched out over the ocean as far as she could see. A gentle west wind meant their journey would be swift and comfortable. She'd replenished her favorite perfume, and Catalina was officially part of the crew. Maybe she was getting the hang of this captain business after all.

Catalina waved from the stairs up to the bridge. "May I join you at the helm for takeoff? I'd like to learn the basic workings of the ship, since I will be here for a time."

A time? How vague. Preparing to leave at a moment's notice, most likely.

Yvette sighed. Everyone left eventually. First her mother, then the Sisters who had claimed to be her friends. At least her father was better off gone. Here on her ship, the whole crew knew they were free to depart to take another job, start a family, settle down to a sedentary life, or whatever else took their fancy. Yvette preferred to pretend they'd all forgotten about that.

"You may join me, but don't touch anything," she told Lina.

The therapist had eschewed any attempt to match the crew uniforms in favor of her own clothing. Today she sported a gray split skirt with navy suspenders over a pale blue top. Her hair was tied up in its usual tight bun. Why did she do that? She had lovely hair. Maybe she didn't like the feel of it blowing in the wind the way Yvette did.

Yvette loved the wind. It gave her a sense of freedom. And when it grew cold enough to sting against her skin, she felt fierce and defiant.

I can take on the world. I am not afraid.

She was afraid, of course. But it was always nice to forget that now and again.

"What is the first step to a takeoff?" Catalina inquired.

Yvette blinked. Back to work. She began naming controls and gauges, showing Lina the fuel level, the water temperature, the steam pressure, and all the other numbers a pilot had to learn to interpret with no more than a glance. Yvette knew the controls so well she could touch each gauge with her eyes closed.

"It's important to check everything at takeoff," she explained. "If your balloon is leaking, you could crash. If your boiler isn't producing enough steam, you could float away at the mercy of the currents. If—"

An explosion swallowed up her words, rocking the airship and leaving her ears ringing.

"Fire!" Angelique shouted. "Fire on the airfield!"

Yvette whirled around to find the source, expecting to see a combusting hydrogen balloon. She filled her ship with helium, despite the higher cost, for exactly this reason.

This time, however, no airships were afire.

"What is that?" Lina asked, scurrying aft for a closer look at the fireball on the ground. The *moving* fireball.

"Nom de dieu!"

Sparks and flames leaped from the iron bed of a cargo truck. A driverless cargo truck headed straight for La Liberté.

"Fly, fly!" Yvette screamed, spinning back toward the controls. "Release the ropes! Go, go, go!" She hammered her fist on the round, flat button at the very top of the controls.

The emergency bell began to clang. All across the deck,

pirates raced to their positions. Yvette flipped switches and grabbed the wheel.

"I thought you said you had to check everything first!" Lina cried.

"No time!"

Screams of terror tore through the air, some from the ground, and some from those on her crew who had seen the danger.

"Get those ropes undone!" she yelled over the chaos.

The fore ropes slackened, and the ship rocked. She dared a glance behind her. Esme had her hands on the last mooring rope, but she moved as if in slow motion, her face a mask of terror. Putain! She had a fear of fire.

"Cut it!" Yvette bellowed so forcefully her throat hurt. "Cut the rope!"

Catalina sprang into action. She raced toward Esme, snatching up one of the emergency hatchets hung along the rail.

"Stand clear! I have this!" she shouted.

Yvette didn't waste time watching. She shoved the throttle up to full power and grabbed the wheel. The ship lurched, straining to break away from the last mooring. Between the shouts, she caught the *thunk* of an axe into something solid. Then a grunt, then another *thunk*.

The rope snapped. La Liberté rocketed into the air, forward and upward at the same time, in the most precarious, reckless ascent Yvette had ever attempted. Her pirates clutched at the rails or tumbled to the deck. The wake from the engines snapped trees and kicked up great clouds of dust. She could get banned from the Savannah airfield for this and lose her most lucrative smuggling contracts.

But they were safe. From the air, Yvette watched the flaming truck race across the empty space where the ship had been, plow through the fence that bordered the airfield, and plunge into the Savannah river. La Liberté was nearing top speed. If this had been a deliberate attack, she had a good head start on anyone who might follow.

Yvette pushed her ship higher and faster, eyes on the dials, feeling the changes in the air and steering to catch the swiftest currents. Her mind had sharpened. There was only this. Only flying. Only escape.

Time slipped away.

"Captain."

The word filtered slowly into Yvette's consciousness. She checked the clock on the controls. Two hours out. Not enough.

"Yvette."

She allowed herself to look at Miss Navarro. The therapist's expression was solemn, but composed. "Yes?"

"Zahra reports no sign of pursuit, but the women are all in agreement that this incident was no accident. They appear to have recovered from the shock, even Clara and Chantal, and are writing up a revised work schedule, focusing on greater speed of travel and enhanced surveillance."

"Good. But why are you telling me this? Zahra will report when she is ready."

Catalina's full lips curved into a wry smile. "Because I think you neglected to tell me everything when you made your… job offer."

Yvette concentrated on the sky ahead of her, still blue and beautiful.

"The attack where Olga was injured wasn't random," Lina continued. "Rescuing the girls wasn't an isolated incident. You have an enemy. An enemy who at the very least knows your usual haunts. You are up to something, and someone wants to stop you."

Denial was pointless. Yvette remained silent.

Catalina leaned close enough that Yvette couldn't ignore

her. Her breath ghosted across Yvette's skin, sending a shiver all the way to her toes.

"Have you lured me into mortal peril, Captain Redbeard?" Lina whispered.

"I keep my people safe." An odd breathiness seeped into Yvette's usual firm tone.

Lina didn't move. Yvette's skin began to heat.

"So loyal," Lina mused. "And yet you hold yourself so very far away. Hiding secrets. Hiding yourself."

Yvette tried to focus on flying, but somehow Catalina had seized hold of her attention and wouldn't give it back.

"You're going to leave, aren't you?"

No one this magnetic would stay. Yvette would be drawn to her, sucked in, until she began to think they would stick forever. Until the magnet flipped and she was thrust away.

Catalina lifted a single finger and stroked it along Yvette's cheek, leaving behind a burning trail of sensation.

"No." she murmured. "I'm not leaving."

She withdrew abruptly, then walked away, calling over her shoulder, "Keep flying. I'll be nearby."

8

$\mathcal{T}$HE CITY OF LIGHT. An apt description, Lina supposed, since electric lights gleamed up from the streets below, slicing through the predawn darkness. She'd heard so much about Paris over the years: its iron tower, the magnificent museums, wondrous exhibitions, infamous brothels, and more. It hardly seemed real, even as the ship descended and the city grew larger and clearer.

The massive airfield rose up beneath her, dotted with dirigibles of all shapes and sizes. La Liberté was only one among dozens arriving or departing.

What on earth am I doing here?

Her stomach couldn't seem to settle, and it wasn't the sway of the airship. Her whole body felt torn between excitement and discomfort. This was a chance to see things she'd always dreamed of, but she was no tourist. She didn't even know why the pirates had come here. Wasn't Paris the site of the attack where Olga had been wounded?

Yvette landed the ship in a remote corner of the airfield, a comfortable distance from any other vessels. The crew, as usual, performed their duties with efficiency and competence, securing the ship and preparing for time on the ground.

The moment they were finished, the whole group gathered

around the captain in the center of the deck. Lina joined them. Though she'd known everyone for almost a week now, she hadn't quite settled in as one of them. Her duties were unusual and sporadic, her place somewhere halfway between crew and guest. Perhaps it always would be.

"As you all know," Yvette stated, with the clear speech of an orator, "when we left the city several days prior, we left a job incomplete. Four girls remain of Clara and Chantal's group, and it is our duty to find them and bring them aboard, where they can decide to join us or be delivered to a safe location."

Heads all around nodded. Lina filed the new information in her mind. The story was becoming clearer, bit by bit, though many gaps remained. A rescue mission had gone wrong. The pirates had returned to finish it. Someone must be paying them well, if they had risked returning to complete the job.

"We will do this quietly," Yvette continued. "Most of you will remain here, unless I send word that we need assistance. Zahra will have command while I am gone. I will lead the search group. Brigid is the stealthiest, so she will join me. Catalina will be our third."

Lina's jaw dropped.

"Everyone to your duties," the captain ordered.

"Aye!" the pirates chorused.

"I…" Lina couldn't get any words out. She had no skills suitable to a rescue mission. She couldn't sneak, couldn't run, couldn't fight. And while she'd received knife training during her university days, it was meant as a surprise defensive maneuver. She could probably save herself. Saving others was beyond her abilities.

She caught the sleeve of Yvette's coat as the captain strode toward the ladder.

"A moment?"

Yvette frowned at her. "What is wrong?"

"Why me?"

The pirate's frown became one of puzzlement. "Because I need you."

A hot shiver of arousal surged through Lina's body.

That's not what she meant. That's not what she meant.

All the reciting in the world couldn't scrub the mental image from Lina's mind: Yvette, spread out before her, pleading for release, begging Lina to be the one to make her lose control.

Lina fought to keep her voice composed. "Why do you need me?"

Yvette placed her hands on her hips and shook her head. "The girls may be afraid, distrustful, confused. You can help them. You will know what to say. Now, let us go. I would like to reach Number Seventeen before the sun is fully risen."

"What's Number Seventeen?" Lina couldn't help asking.

"My mother's residence." Yvette waved a nonchalant hand and swung herself over the rail onto the ladder.

· · • ☕ • · ·

Number Seventeen was a brothel.

"Not the first famous Parisian sight I'd expected to see," Lina murmured.

She didn't mind being wrong. The lobby was an elegant, sumptuous delight, full of lush fabrics, gilded accessories, and beautiful ladies. Lina could imagine settling onto one of the plush cushions, sipping a perfect French coffee, and admiring the scenery.

"One of my mother's girls is a contact," Yvette explained. She scanned the room, then waved.

A buxom brunette clad only in tiny lace knickers and a matching top scurried over to them. The scraps of lace concealed almost nothing, but definitely drew attention to the relevant areas. Lina gave the woman a thorough perusal and an appreciative grin. The brunette canted her hips and blew Lina a flirtatious kiss.

Yvette scowled. "We are not here for that, Mimi. I need

information. I'm searching for a woman and four adolescent girls from a Swiss boarding school. Last seen ten days ago."

"Hmm." The scantily clad woman straightened and pursed her lips. "You expect them to be together?"

"I couldn't say. They were with us during an attack. I didn't see any of them go down, but I was unable to follow when they ran."

The brunette tossed her curls. "I've heard nothing of any adult woman. But I did hear mention a few days ago about foreign girls hiding below."

Yvette bounced, a single up-down motion that Lina now recognized as an expression of pleasure.

"Thank you." Yvette tossed Mimi a gold coin. "If you or anyone else hears anything different, leave me a note." She spun around and gestured at Brigid and Lina. "Come. We're going below."

Lina jogged to match the pirate's rapid strides. "What or where is 'below'?" For God's sake, could the woman be any more sparse with information?

"The sewers."

Lina almost stumbled. She looked down at her neatly-pressed split skirt and her perfectly clean hands. Sewers were for rats and garbage. Not for scientists. Not for her.

Yvette and Brigid strode down the street as casually as everyone else out at this time of morning. Lina trailed slightly behind, her mind awhirl.

She hadn't joined a pirate crew, she'd joined some kind of circus troupe. She was the straight man baffled by the antics of the clowns. And this day had barely begun.

"Why did I ever agree to this job?" she muttered. She'd been suckered in by the promise of analytical study of a group of interesting and independent women. Or perhaps she was the victim of her lust-addled brain, which kept wishing Yvette would remove her long coat to better display the swing of her hips. Probably both.

"What did you say?" Yvette asked, not turning around.

Lina had had enough. She couldn't continue on, never knowing what was happening. "I need more information. You two may make excursions into the sewers on a daily basis, but I assure you I do not. I need details. Where are we going? How are we to get there? What should I expect once we are 'below'? If I am to be part of this crew, you can't continue to leave me in the dark. And you can't drag me into a cesspool without explanation!"

Yvette slowed to allow Lina to step into place at her left side. "The sewers aren't terrible, the way you might think. They are new and modern. They mimic the city streets and provide excellent pathways for smuggling, evading enemies, and hiding. I—and most of the crew—can navigate the tunnels as easily as the streets above. The girls we are looking for will have some knowledge of the sewers, including certain particular hiding places."

And exactly how *do schoolgirls have such knowledge?* Lina wanted to ask. But she didn't dare disrupt Yvette's explanation. Incomplete explanations were better than none.

"We will join a tour boat," the captain continued. "People come from all over to see the fine technology we have here in Paris." Unmistakable pride filled her voice.

"This is your birthplace?" Lina guessed. Blast. So much for not interrupting.

"Oui," Yvette answered. "I belong to the greatest city in the world."

Brigid sniffed.

"Don't mind her." Yvette waved a hand. "She is German. She doesn't understand."

Brigid grumbled something vulgar in her native language, making Yvette laugh.

"The tour boat?" Lina asked, attempting to steer the conversation back on track.

Yvette nodded. "When we reach the desired location, we

will leave the boat and I will lead us through the tunnels to the most likely places to find the girls. If we find them, we lead them back to the ship. If not, we will need to seek more information. Does that satisfy you?"

I won't be satisfied until you tell me things without prompting. Until you trust me with all the things you still don't say. Until you show me who you are and why you hide.

"Yes," Lina replied. "It does."

9

Yvette tucked her hair up under her tricorn cap and buttoned her coat to hide her chest. She'd passed for a boy hundreds of times. No one would take any notice of her.

Brigid, who already wore her hair short, had donned a newsboy cap. She was too buxom to hide her figure easily, but she was young enough to adopt the persona of a rebellious teenage girl. Catalina, with her prim, perfect bun and tidy clothing, could play the role of governess.

Yvette discreetly dropped a few coins into Lina's hand. "You pay. You are the teacher and we are your unruly charges."

"I don't speak French," Lina protested.

Yvette simply nudged her toward the ticket counter outside the narrow entrance to the sewers below.

"Trois billets?" asked the ticket seller, glancing only briefly at their group before reaching for the tickets.

Lina nodded, set the money on the counter, then glared at Yvette.

Yvette grinned back. Perfect. Stuffy governess and scamp of a boy.

The trio trudged down the stairs, where a group of tourists had gathered, chattering and pointing at the large sewer tunnel in front of them. The brick and concrete corridor had a smooth, curved roof, with small pipes and a string of dim electric lights running along its length. Narrow walkways flanked the shallow river that carried sludge safely away from the Seine and the city's drinking water.

Here in the main channel, the smell was only strong enough to give the tourists the thrill of visiting someplace dirty and forbidden. Lina, of course, was already wrinkling her nose and grimacing. She would get used to it.

Yvette led the others into the back row of the small barge that would float down the tunnel for the tour. Most of the group chose the front, where they would be closer to the dragon that pulled the boat, flapping its steel wings and huffing steam. Slipping away would be child's play.

"People do this for *fun*?" Lina hissed, as the boat glided down the tunnel.

Overhead, the lights grew dimmer and further apart. At the front of the vehicle, the tour guide gushed about the brilliance of the design, the forward-thinking technologies, and the cleanliness of the city. Lina didn't appear to understand a word. Yvette would have to begin French lessons with her.

"I think it's interesting." Brigid smiled broadly, looking all around her. "I studied engineering. I would like to build something like this one day."

Yvette toyed with the small torch in her pocket, flicking it on and off repeatedly. Waiting was always agonizing. Yet it was a part of so many missions. Every time, it was a struggle to keep her mind on the task, when all she wanted was to daydream away the tedium.

On, off, on, off, twist, spin, on, off. At least her hands could keep busy.

At long last, the passage Yvette wanted appeared up ahead on the left-side wall. She nudged her companions and pointed.

Lina tensed beside her. The therapist disliked this, but she wouldn't voice her opinion. She hadn't run, hadn't demanded a different option.

Yvette gave her a proud smile. Catalina made a good pirate. She faced down her fears and fought through discomfort. She listened to orders, but spoke up when she didn't understand or when she disagreed. She could become an important contributor to the team.

As long as she didn't get distracted flirting with all the pretty girls. Yvette scowled again, remembering the way Lina had eyed Mimi. Such behavior ought to be confined to personal time. And certainly not done in front of the captain.

The boat had nearly reached the side tunnel. Yvette gave her companions a nod. One-by-one, they climbed from the barge and slipped into the smaller passageway, stealthy Brigid bringing up the rear.

"No one saw me," she reported.

Yvette led the way into the darkness, walking with one hand on the wall to prevent her from stumbling into the muck in the center channel. Lina's fingers dug into the back of her coat.

"You don't need to hold me," Yvette whispered. "Just put a hand on the wall."

Lina's grip relaxed, then finally slipped away. "This is revolting! And the smell is growing worse."

"You will live." The sounds of the tour boat had faded, so Yvette flicked on her torch to illuminate their path. She turned to Lina. "Better?"

Lina yanked her hand off the wall, shaking it, as if that could dislodge any foul substances. "Those girls had better be down here."

"They will be," Brigid said confidently. "It is where I would go."

"How do the girls know about these tunnels?" Lina asked.

"They learn at school. We were taught many practical things when I was there."

Yvette kicked at a loose piece of rock, sending it splashing into the water. She hadn't been sent to school. Her father would have had to part with an inconsequential amount of his plunder for that.

"Interesting school," Lina mused.

Yvette lifted a finger to her lips. "No more talking. It is time to begin the search and we don't want anyone to know we are here."

Lina nodded and followed soundlessly as their trek resumed. She had a sensible head. And already she'd adjusted to the smell. She truly had a knack for pirating. If only there was a way to convince her to give up her boring, orderly life forever.

Everyone leaves.

Yvette tried to pull her thoughts back on track. It was a very good thing she could navigate these tunnels automatically.

The next turn took them into a small passageway, where they had to duck and straddle the center channel in order to fit. Lina made a soft grumbling sound, but remained faithfully at Yvette's back.

"Only a few more turns," Yvette whispered.

She led the group down another narrow tunnel, then a third. The smuggling hold she aimed for had been her father's favorite, in part because of the small, winding route to get there. That, and the proximity of the sewer drain to his dismal, but opulent, residence.

Yvette held up a hand to signal to her companions, and everyone came to a halt. She clicked off the torch and returned it to her pocket.

"No light, no sound," she whispered. "Stay here. I will take a look, then return."

Yvette stepped out into the next intersection and turned left. Ahead, the sewer widened into a storage area and access point for maintenance. A light flickered in the far right corner. Her girls?

She crept closer. A hacking cough echoed off the concrete

walls, the pitch much too low to be a young woman. A man's grumbled curse soon followed.

Yvette backed away, one hand delving beneath her coat to clasp her knife. These men could be remnants of her father's crew, possibly the same miscreants behind the attack ten days ago.

She barely breathed until she made it around the corner to where Lina and Brigid waited.

"Ruffians," she whispered. "Brigid, lead the way to hold C." She clicked the torch on and passed it up to Brigid.

Brigid, who had been navigating the sewers almost as long as Yvette, set a swift pace through the criss-crossing corridors.

"I have no idea where we are," Lina fretted. "Please don't leave me."

Yvette almost stumbled. Level-headed, tough Miss Navarro having a moment of vulnerability? A grin tugged at Yvette's mouth. It was oddly sweet seeing Lina unafraid to admit to her fears.

"We won't leave you." She laid a hand on Lina's shoulder, giving a gentle squeeze of reassurance.

Lina leaned into the touch, a tiny sigh escaping her lips as her muscles relaxed beneath Yvette's hand.

Yvette jumped back. She was the captain. She couldn't let anyone think her soft. "Pirates work as a team," she said brusquely. "We leave no woman behind." She stabbed a finger toward the street signs marking the next intersection. "The sewers follow the streets. You can always find where you are."

Better. Properly piratical.

Yvette flexed her fingers, trying to ease the tingles her brief touch had left behind. It didn't work. Inside her chest, her heart was all aflutter. Lina's sigh played on a loop in her mind. The glimpse of Sweet Lina was like a tray of the most decadent sweets; she craved more, more, so much more. Her entire body had become tingles and sighs and a terrifying tremble of excitement.

Bordel!

Yvette knew how it felt to have her heart broken. To be abandoned again and again by those she loved. If her own mother hadn't wanted her, why would anyone else? She could not, would not, put her heart at risk. She would choose criminals lurking in sewers over Lina's sort of danger any day.

10

I MAKE A HORRIBLE PIRATE.

Lina focused on Brigid's movements, putting one foot in front of another, determined not to succumb to another moment of weakness, even if she had to spend another hour in these dark and disgusting sewer tunnels.

Keep to the task. Keep walking.

No matter how she concentrated, Yvette's phantom touch lingered on her shoulder. So delicate. So tender.

Her imagination was running amok. Yvette had only been concerned Lina might swoon. It was a logical assumption, given the stench and her obvious display of fear. Longing for a gentler response than gruff words about pirates and street signs didn't make it real.

"Fast da," Brigid said, then a moment later added, "Almost there."

Lina repeated the German phrase in her head a few times. She needed to start learning at least small amounts of the many tongues spoken by the multi-lingual pirates.

Up ahead, the tunnel ended at a t-shaped intersection. Yvette let out a soft whistle a few yards short of the turn. Brigid halted so abruptly Lina had to pull back to avoid colliding with her.

Which, naturally, meant she collided with Yvette instead. The captain's entire body slammed into hers. Lina's instinct was to wiggle her hips and press closer. Fortunately, the contact lasted only a second, freeing her from any need to restrain herself.

"Pardon," Yvette said, then mumbled in a tone half-flirtatious, half-cynical, "Quelle belle derriere."

Lina almost whirled around, the words "Did you just say what I thought you said?" on the tip of her tongue.

"Brigid." Yvette cut off Lina's chance with her whispered command. "Turn off the light, then go around the corner and sneak to hold C. If the girls are there, do not scare them. Return and report whatever you find."

"Aye," Brigid replied.

The tunnel went dark.

Without her eyesight, Lina's other senses sprang to high alert. The smell of sewage grew stronger. When she reached out to steady herself, the rough brick abraded her fingers. Her ears caught every tiny noise: the ripple of slowing moving water, the distant scuttle of rats, the rustle of cloth as Yvette shifted behind her.

Lina's breath caught. Those brief touches had been nothing. Inconsequential. Yet they had left her attuned to Yvette most of all. Her ears strained to catch even the slightest movement, or the soft inhalation of a breath. She felt impossibly close and painfully far away at the same time.

Anything could happen in the darkness. Things that could be forgotten in the light of day.

Lina reached to put her left hand on the wall, needing the grounding of both hands against solid brick.

Her fingers brushed Yvette's. Lina let out a gasp, half surprise, half excitement.

This time, Yvette didn't pull away. She covered Lina's hand with her own and kept it there. Warm. Soft.

Lina's pulse pounded in her ears. Yvette's touch could be

nothing more than a gesture of comfort. A sign of solidarity. Still, possibility burned in her mind as hot as the skin-to-skin contact. Could it also be an overture of friendship? Or an amorous proposition?

What do you want it to be, Catalina?

She honestly didn't know. Her body craved sexual pleasure, naturally, but she'd had years of practice confining that to appropriate situations. Her mind, however, couldn't quite seem to choose. An affair would be nice. So would friendship. Comfort, certainly. Yet each seemed strangely lacking.

Lina didn't move. She would enjoy this moment for whatever it was, even if the true reason was Yvette trying to prevent her from screaming or running off.

Time became meaningless. In this dark, silent place, they simply existed. Two people, together. Cut off from the usual flow of time and space, but not alone.

Brigid returned eventually, her flashlight cutting through the darkness and shifting the world back into focus. Yvette released Lina's hand, but the sense of connection remained. This would alter their relationship. For the better, Lina hoped.

"The girls are there," Brigid reported. "They are hidden behind empty crates, scraps of wood, whatever they could find. And they are armed."

"Knives? Pistols?" Yvette asked.

"Clumsy weapons. Sticks and pipes. They are scared."

"They must believe an enemy is searching for them," Lina mused. "Or even that their location is known. We will need to take care when we approach them."

Finally, finally, the time had come to use her talents. No more uncertainty or hesitation. This was what Catalina Navarro, psychological therapist, had been born to do.

"If we startle them, they may lash out," she continued. "If that happens, we cannot respond in any way that could be seen as threatening. They likely don't know who to trust, even if they recognize you. You two should take protective positions, as if looking to fend off approaching enemies. I will address the girls and calm them as best as I can. Will they understand English?"

"All girls from the Illyrian Institute speak German, French, and English," Brigid said proudly.

Yvette looked away to hide a scowl. Curious. "Lead the way," she commanded.

The hideout wasn't far. Brigid kept the flashlight on, pointed at the ground. Soon, the tunnel widened, revealing a rectangular storage area. The barricade the girls had constructed emerged from the darkness. They could surely see the light now, and would be ready to defend themselves.

"Tell them we are here," Lina whispered to Yvette. "Before we step out into the possible line of fire."

"Brigid, take a position here and guard our back." Yvette didn't shout, but her voice carried well in the confined space. "I will cross to the other side to guard against threat from ahead. Catalina, I will leave you to your work." She strode off, bold as anything, directly past the barricade.

For a moment, Lina couldn't breathe. This wasn't any group of school girls. These young women were clearly resourceful, knowledgeable in the areas of defense and survival, and almost certainly terrified. What would stop them from attacking first and asking questions later?

Yvette showed no sign of fear. She put her back to the barricade, peering down the tunnel for any signs of trouble.

"Girls from the Illyrian Institute?" Lina called out in the same gentle voice she'd used with Clara. "We are the crew of La Liberté." She steeled herself, then stepped out into the open. "I'm Lina, a friend of Clara and Chantal. I would like to take you to them, if you are willing."

Murmured voices and shuffling noises rose from behind the pile of debris.

Lina stepped closer. "Are you able to come out?" She held up both hands. "I am unarmed." Not entirely true, but no one needed to know that.

More murmuring, just loud enough for Lina to recognize that it wasn't English.

"If anyone is injured or ill, my friends can assist you. The crew of La Liberté leaves no woman behind. That is why we've come back for you."

The girls hadn't attacked—and showed no signs of doing so. Lina's professional instincts said they were no danger to her. She listened and climbed over the barricade.

Behind her, Yvette cursed in French.

Lina ignored it. She was in her element now. She could handle this.

The four girls sat huddled on the floor, a sad, bedraggled mess in the near darkness. They clutched makeshift weapons. The scent of recently-burned oil wafted from the unlit lamp at their feet.

"I understand there are enemies after you," Lina said gently. "You must be so scared. I'm scared too. I've only been in these sewers for part of a morning, and all I can think about is getting out so I can wash and fill my belly with hot food. I know it's worse for you. I want to take you away from here, but I want it to be your choice." She extended a hand. "I can only offer. The decision is yours."

Lina waited, considering next steps for comforting and gaining trust. A few seconds later, one of the girls reached out to take Lina's hand.

"I would like to be with Clara and Chantal," she whispered.

Lina helped her to her feet. "I promise I will take you to them. And get you a bath and a hot meal and a soft blanket to wrap up in."

"Thank you." The girl looked down at the others and nodded. "We will all go."

The other three climbed to their feet, clustering behind their leader.

"Keep your weapons, if it helps you," Lina suggested. "We

will not leave anyone behind, but holding hands may ease some of the fear of becoming separated."

The leader of the girls squeezed Lina's hand, dropped her cudgel, and held out a hand to the girl nearest to her. The rest of the girls linked hands, with only the girl in the rear keeping her iron rod. This last girl was tall, broad in the shoulders, and buxom. A strong, powerful woman, despite her obvious fear. She'd deliberately placed herself at the rear of the group. These girls were smart, loyal, and knew how to use their skills to help the group. They would make brilliant pirates.

Lina kicked aside some of the debris and led the girls through their barricade. Yvette's smile of delight made her stop in her tracks.

"Well done, Catalina! I knew you were exactly right for helping our girls." Yvette broke into rapid French. Lina didn't understand the words, but gathered that Yvette was re-introducing herself to the girls and explaining what happened next. "The closest exit is this way," she finished in English, pointing the opposite direction from the way they'd entered.

Brigid passed Yvette the flashlight, then positioned herself at the rear of the group, giving an appreciative nod to the girl with the weapon.

Lina kept close behind Yvette as the group started off. "The airship is stocked with a vast array of soaps and perfumes," she said quietly, hoping to keep up the morale of the group with talk of the nice things awaiting them. "Fruits, flowers, spices."

Lina continued as they trudged on, detailing the different bath and beauty products. After that, she turned to the variety of excellent foods in La Liberté's galley. The hand gripping hers had relaxed, a good sign the girls were growing more comfortable.

"There are even cookies," she added cheerfully. "Flakey lemon cookies dusted with sugar. The captain's favorite. She has a fondness for sweets and loves to share them with her friends."

"How do you know—" Yvette cut off abruptly and held up a hand to stop the group. She cocked her head, frowning.

It took Lina a moment to catch what had startled Yvette. A rumbling, crunching sound, faint but growing louder. An additional whooshing noise began to emerge. Rushing water?

Yvette lifted the flashlight and pointed it straight down the tunnel, illuminating a dozen-or-so yards ahead of them.

The sounds grew louder.

"Back," Yvette ordered. "Go back."

And then Lina saw it. An iron ball, as large as the tunnel, hurtling toward them.

She spun, dragging the chain of girls with her.

"Run!"

11

Commands rang out in a flurry of languages. Yvette shouted as she ran, pushing the pack of young women ahead of her.

"Allez!"

"Geht doch!"

"Go! Hurry!"

"Schnell!"

Brigid's voice was shrill. One of the girls was screaming. The rumbling of the accursed sewer ball increased steadily.

"Faster!" Lina urged. "You can do it! There's a turn not far from your hideout!"

Brigid splashed down into the shallow channel of sewage. Despite the ankle-deep water, she ran faster than she had on the narrow lip above.

"Schnell!" she called again.

Two of the girls immediately followed her. A third hesitated, lost her footing, and tumbled to her knees in the muck.

Yvette's hand shot out, ready to haul the girl to her feet, but Lina was already there, leaping into the sewage as if she no longer cared what foul things lurked down here. She grabbed the girl under the arms to help her up.

Yvette seized the arm of the last girl and helped her around her fallen comrade and into the water. "Run!"

The girl took off and Yvette dared to glance behind.

"Nom de Dieu!"

The tumbling ball was no more than five meters away. Lina and the girl were still struggling to stand.

"Yvette, run!" Lina shouted.

Yvette couldn't move. She was the captain. Her duty was to protect her crew. Letting anyone else fall behind was unthinkable.

Lina steadied the girl on her feet, then propelled her forward. "Catch your friends and you get the first bath!" She snatched hold of Yvette's arm, the one holding the torch, causing the light to dance wildly about the tunnel. "Hurry up, damn you!"

Yvette ran. She was faster than Lina, and soon she was pushing from behind rather than being dragged along. Filthy water flew with every pounding stride, splashing her clothes, her face, her hands. Crushing, crunching sounds screamed in her ears, along with the roar of the water that propelled the ball onward.

They raced past the girls' hideout. The rush of water ceased, as the stream spread through the wider space, but the momentum of the iron ball kept it tumbling along at a furious pace. Lina splashed forward, arms flailing, her footing unsure on the wet brick—not yet accustomed to the perils of pirate life.

"Faster!" Yvette snarled, hoping the demand would spark Lina's anger and give her the boost she needed.

The side tunnel appeared at the end of the flashlight's range. Brigid and the girls disappeared safely around the corner. Almost there.

Yvette took one last look over her shoulder and nearly screamed. She could see her death coming: the massive iron monster slamming into her, crushing her bones, leaving her a broken heap in the sewage, where she would either bleed out or drown.

No, no, no.

She couldn't let it happen to her. She couldn't let it happen to Lina. They were close, so close, but the ball was faster and nearly at their heels.

Only a few meters left. She could get Lina around the corner with a well-timed shove.

"I'm going to push you!" Yvette shouted, putting all her body weight into propelling the other woman up and to the right. Lina half-flew, half-leapt into the side tunnel. Safe.

Yvette tried to spin to follow, but her forward inertia was too much. She stumbled and fell, sprawling on her stomach, only one arm out of the path of the onrushing sphere.

Now, she did scream, her last chance before her body was crushed and her breath stolen permanently away.

A pair of hands clamped down on her arm, fingernails digging into her flesh. What a minor pain, compared to what was about to happen.

"No. Woman. Left. Behind!" Lina roared, yanking Yvette with such force that her arm nearly popped out of the socket.

Yvette sailed up off the sewer floor, landing in Catalina's lap at the exact moment the deadly sewer ball crashed past.

For several seconds she lay where she was, gasping for air. Sacré Dieu, Lina was so soft beneath her. Warm. Comforting. Yvette wanted to clutch her tightly and weep into the cushion of her breasts.

Captains did not weep.

"No woman left behind," Lina whispered, running a gentle hand over Yvette's wet, tangled hair.

Her hat was lost to the sewers. She'd loved that hat. Tears began to fall. Lina's hand kept stroking. She was so very kind. A truly good person.

Yvette slipped from Lina's grasp and pushed herself to her feet. The tears were a steady stream now, but she ignored them. Captains didn't weep, and everyone left her. Her heart must remain untouched.

The torch flickered where she'd dropped it in the murky

water. She fished it out, shook it semi-dry, then pointed it down the tunnel.

She addressed the group in her captain's voice. "We will return the way we came. Quickly and quietly. We *will* be out of here soon. I swear it on my life."

And without another word, she strode off, ushering the cluster of sodden, exhausted women with her. Duty called.

12

EVEN IN PARIS, stripping to one's underthings before boarding a dirigible was a scandalous act. Yvette gave the order anyway, and not a single woman complained. They unceremoniously dropped the sewer-drenched garments in a rubbish heap, then climbed aboard La Liberté.

Clara and Chantal rushed to greet their friends, ushering them off to the bathing chamber to clean and recover. The bath only held four. Yvette, Lina, and Brigid would have to wait.

There was no sense wasting time. Yvette saw to her duties straightaway, preparing for takeoff and getting the ship safely into the air. Captaining an airship in only a chemise and drawers was hardly the oddest thing she'd done in her life.

Time passed quickly as she flew, as it always did. But when the girls were finished, Yvette didn't hesitate to pass the helm to Zahra. She hurried below deck to join Lina and Brigid as they enveloped themselves in warm, foamy delight.

Yvette had spent an enormous sum of money on the luxurious bathing chamber, and not once had she regretted it. Today, she was even more convinced of the soundness of her investment. Gloriously hot water streamed down from the rainshower spouts above, stirring up the fragrant bubbles on the floor of the massive tiled bathtub. She was in heaven.

The mingled scents of lemon and roses wafted through the steamy air, tickling her nose in much the same way as the bubbles tickled her feet. Catalina's soaps were magnificent: pleasing to the nose, gentle on the skin, and effective at removing whatever dirt and grime a lady pirate might encounter on her adventures.

Brigid turned her back to Lina. "Scrub my back?"

A pang of loneliness twinged in Yvette's chest. Brigid's question wasn't merely a request for help. It was a gesture of bonding among the crew. A sign you trusted the other woman not to stab you when you were at your most vulnerable.

Yvette never participated. Not that she believed any of her crew would do her harm. But self-reliance was her most vital defense. If everything fell apart, she had to know she could take care of herself.

Lina soaped up Brigid's back, humming a cheerful little tune. "Would you like me to wash your hair as well?" she asked.

Yvette had to turn away when Lina plunged her fingers into Brigid's short locks. She remembered the feel of those hands all too well. Gentle fingers stroking her hair after her close call with the sewer ball. The softest of caresses, as if she were delicate and precious.

She scrubbed her own hair with abrupt, vigorous strokes. If there was any delicacy left in her, she would scour it away.

When the last of the dirt was rinsed away, Yvette closed the drain and let the tub begin to fill. She'd washed off the grime and the smell, but if she wanted to cleanse herself of the strain of her brush with death, she needed a hot soak and plenty more bubbles.

Brigid hopped out of the tub and grabbed a towel. "No bath for me. I do not want to become wrinkly like a raisin. I will check on the girls and find them clothes and bunks. You two can rest from our adventure." She swung the towel around herself and slipped out the door.

Yvette sank down into the water, leaning back against the tiles and stretching her legs out. Steamy water rose over her legs and crept up her torso. She grabbed a small bottle of bubble oil from the ledge and poured a generous amount into the tub.

Lina took a seat beside her. "So this is a pirate's life? Pillage and plunder, then bubble bath?"

"Naturellement. We are *ladies*."

Yvette stirred the water with one foot, creating a pretty pile of suds. In reality, she was the furthest thing from a lady. Her mother was a whore and her father was a thief and murderer. Even some of the Daughters of Redbeard had looked down their noses at her.

But on her ship, none of it mattered. Here, everyone had nice things, warm baths, and hot meals, regardless of where they'd come from. She reached behind her and turned the handle to stop the flow of water before the bubbles could rise past her shoulders.

"I like that," Lina replied. "I think it's refreshing that you all can enjoy pretty, feminine things, while flying airships and rescuing damsels in distress." She leaned back and closed her eyes. The position made her back arch, thrusting her breasts up above the bubbles.

Yvette did not stare at those soft, lush mounds. Absolutely not. Nor did she contemplate blowing a handful of suds in Lina's direction to see if she could make a bubble pop on one of those taut, dark nipples. Ladies didn't do such things.

Except she was also a pirate. And pirates liked buxom wenches and breaking rules.

Lina was still talking. Something about women and expected roles. Yvette hadn't meant to stop paying attention. She never did. Her brain simply wandered elsewhere, until she realized she'd missed a portion of the conversation, and then had to smile and say something vague.

She skimmed a palmful of bubbles off the surface of the water and blew gently on them, popping a few and merging others into larger and larger bubbles.

"...considered unladylike..." Lina said.

Yvette sent the bubbles flying into the air. The soapy orbs danced and glittered with rainbow light, drifting downward until they burst in tiny explosions of droplets.

"…idea of feminine behavior is a social construct…"

Yvette blew another handful of bubbles. "People should be who they want to be," she replied. Or maybe interrupted.

"Exactly." Lina sat up and opened her eyes. "You can like swords *and* bubble baths."

Yvette nodded as she blew a soft stream of air into her cupped hands. The bubble popped, so she began again.

"You can marry and have babies or not marry and not have babies, or any combination thereof."

"I don't like babies," Yvette murmured. She formed another bubble between her fingers, blowing it larger and larger until the pop splashed on her face. "But I would adopt an older child."

"Another valid choice. That's all we really want, is choice. People of any gender should be allowed to do what they want, dress how they want, love whom they want. I might wear a dress to woo ladies. You might wear trousers to woo men."

"Or both." Yvette's efforts paid off at last. Large, round, and dazzling, the beautiful bubble floated out across the water, then landed on the tiled lip of the tub in a perfect dome. Ha! Triumph!

She swept a hand through the foam to try again, then paused when she realized Lina had stopped talking.

Bubbles dripped from between Yvette's fingers. Drat. What had she done now? She shifted slightly to look at Lina.

Heat shimmered in Lina's dark eyes. Her gaze moved leisurely over Yvette's body, lingering on her mouth and on the rounded tops of her small breasts, just visible above the surface. Lina licked her lips.

The rest of the world suddenly ceased to exist. Heat burned through Yvette, though her body appeared frozen in place. She was going to drown in Lina's molten gaze. Where was the drain? Wasn't there a drain here? She needed to get rid of this scorching water or her crew would find her dead on the tiles.

"You like both, don't you, Yvette?" Catalina murmured.

Words wouldn't come. Yvette's tongue felt thick. Had she been poisoned?

"Do you like *me*?" Lina tilted forward, her lips slightly parted.

A switch flipped in Yvette's brain, and her voice began to work again. "If I'm poisoned, I may as well die happy."

"Wh—"

Yvette cut off Lina's question with a kiss.

At last.

Her entire body unclenched. This was what she'd truly been craving since that moment in the sewers in Lina's arms. A taste of sweetness. A gentle touch. A certainty that she was alive and whole and desirable.

Lina's lips were soft and pliant. She made no move to try to wrest control away, as some of Yvette's past lovers had done. She simply let Yvette take her time to taste and explore.

Glorious.

Yvette lingered in every sensation, tracing Lina's lips with her tongue, sucking gently, then easing them apart. She cupped Lina's face in her hands, adjusting their positions until their mouths were perfectly aligned. Tongues stroked tongues. Breath mingled with breath. Every movement unhurried, soothing.

In a life where everything seemed chaotic and overstimulating, this kiss was ecstasy. A blissful escape. A moment of serenity.

And mon Dieu, was it sensual. Her mind had relaxed, but her body buzzed with electricity. It was as if the languid friction of lips and tongues was building to a sudden static jolt.

The jolt came, in the form of Lina's hands tangling in Yvette's hair. The kiss became frantic then, desperate—a quest to gather as much as they could of one another before time ran out.

Lina was the one to pull back. "The water's getting cold."

Yvette had no reply. She remained trapped in the feel of the kiss, the tingle in her lips and the lingering taste of Lina blocking out all other sensations.

"Also, my stomach is growling. Shall we dry off and have something to eat? And look in on the girls?"

Food. Girls. Ugh. She was being a bad captain again, forgetting about everything.

"Oui." Yvette reached to open the drain.

Lina leaned in to give her a peck on the cheek before climbing from the tub. "Thank you for the kiss. It was lovely. I don't know what your rules are regarding intimate relations aboard ship, but if it's permissible, I would be happy to arrange another time—for kissing and beyond, if you'd like."

Yvette stared dazedly at Lina as she toweled off. What, exactly, had they just done? And moreover, what did it mean?

The only thing she could think to say was, "There are no rules."

13

*L*INA HUDDLED BENEATH the wool cloak, glad the voluminous hood concealed her features. She didn't need the other women seeing how much she hated flying in this weather.

More thunder rumbled. They'd altered course to fly around the massive stormcloud, but a steady rain still pelted the ship. Lightning flashed in the distance. A gust of wind tore the hood from Lina's head.

"Damn wind," she growled. No need to watch her language here. A definite benefit of living with pirates.

She plodded toward the prow, where the girls had gathered. No one had asked her to check on them, but Lina couldn't countenance hiding below in her warm, dry room. The crew had welcomed her as one of them, and she was determined to show her solidarity.

Even through the rain, Lina could see tension in the expressions and postures the girls had adopted. They'd been resilient these past twenty-four hours, but this spate of nasty weather was the sort of thing that could tip a person under stress over the edge.

"It still won't be safe," griped a pale, freckled English girl named Susan.

"Hush," chided Ursula, the group leader. "No one will

know where we've gone. We will be able to do as we please. Or join the pirates and help rescue everyone else from the Institute."

"*Pfft.* They're *pirates.* They only did this for the money. I wish we'd stayed at school. It wasn't so bad."

"Fraulein Seidel abandoned us," Ursula retorted. "And maybe led us into a trap."

Susan tossed back her hood and put her hands on her hips. "No one attacked us at school. The pirates will probably murder us in our sleep."

Clara leapt in front of her. "Take that back! They saved us and put their own lives at risk doing it. They are great women!"

Susan snorted. "They're nothing but a bunch of thieves."

Clara shoved her.

Lina broke into a run.

"We could have made something of ourselves!" Susan returned the shove, knocking Clara to the ground. "Instead of rotting in the middle of nowhere!"

Clara scrambled to her feet and lunged at Susan, grabbing a fistful of hair. Susan let out a screech.

"Enough!" Lina grabbed each girl by the arm, trying to drag them apart.

With only two hands, her intervention was minimal. The girls kicked and punched and snatched at one another's clothes and hair, shouting with every blow.

"Von Arx is corrupt!" Clara bellowed. "She cares nothing for us! She had us 'study' in that horrible dungeon, when really she was using us to build machines for Redbeard!"

Lina couldn't make heads or tails of the argument. Machines? Von Arx? Dungeon? She was sorely lacking in basic information regarding these pirates, the Institute, and their history.

"Girls, stop!" she ordered. First things first. Her questions could come later.

Ursula and the others joined Lina, and together they managed to pull Susan and Clara apart.

Susan tried one last futile swing at her opponent. "So you hated Redbeard, but you join his daughter?" She sneered, letting her gaze drift up and down Clara's blue and white pirate uniform.

Clara let her hands drop and straightened her spine. "She is *different*. These pirates are different. They care about more than themselves, and I am proud to join them." Her friends had relaxed their grips enough that she easily shook loose. "Now I am going to go do my job." She turned her back on Susan and stalked off. Chantal raced after her.

Lina steered Susan away from the rest of the group. She kept her voice low, letting the steady patter of rain lend some privacy. "You will never be required to join the crew," she stated firmly. "Nor will you be required to remain anywhere we take you. This is only to keep you all safe. We want you to have the opportunity to choose your own life and not be forced into anything by anyone."

The girl huffed. "I wish I'd stayed at school."

"Well, if the school is safe, I'm sure we can arrange to return you there. Or we can find you another school. Perhaps a university."

Lina sincerely hoped she wasn't misleading the girl. She needed to have a long talk with Yvette. If she didn't know the history behind all this mayhem, how was she supposed to work with these girls?

Susan huffed again, then turned to walk away.

"You're not going to fight again?" Lina asked, infusing her tone with a hint of warning.

"I won't fight," Susan sighed. She ran to the stairs and disappeared below deck.

Lina adjusted her cloak—perhaps she could keep some small portion of herself dry—and walked up to the bridge where Yvette was piloting the ship. She didn't want to disrupt the captain while she was dodging a storm, but this matter needed to be dealt with as soon as possible.

"We need to talk," Lina stated. No embellishments, no pleas, just the straightforward truth. "I will await you in your cabin. Join me as soon as it is safe to do so." She nodded to Yvette, then went below to dry off.

· · · ☕ · · ·

Lina lay on her back, eyes closed, savoring the softness of Yvette's bed. She nearly dozed off, but the sound of the door jolted her to alertness. Yvette had arrived at last.

While Lina lurched to a sitting position, Yvette closed the door and turned up the lamp. She was soaked from head to toe, her shirt and vest plastered to her torso and her sodden trousers hanging low on her hips. Strands of wet hair had come loose from her plait, and droplets glistened on her eyelashes. Half bedraggled waif, half siren.

Yvette bent to remove her boots. "I need to change clothes. You may begin talking."

Lina's brain took a moment to reorient itself. Right. She was here for information.

"Actually, I need you to talk," she replied. "I've realized I don't know enough about your situation or that of the girls we rescued to properly work with them. I feel as if I'm always a step behind. What is the Illyrian Institute? Who is von Arx? What is the connection to you?"

"Ah." Leaving her boots by the door, Yvette padded over to the closet to grab dry clothing. "So that is what you wanted." She sounded oddly surprised.

"Yes. Everyone else on board is familiar with the situation, or parts of it. I'm still confused about everything."

Yvette unbuttoned her vest and began to do the same to her shirt. Lina kept her eyes deliberately focused elsewhere. She would let nothing distract her until she learned what she needed.

"The Illyrian Institute for the Education of Exceptional Young Women is an exclusive school in the Alps," Yvette explained. "Many rich Europeans send their daughters there—the eccentric or 'unladylike' daughters. Headmistress von Arx oversees their admission and education. Her motivations are… questionable, and she works to indoctrinate the students to her cause."

Lina slid to the edge of the bed, letting her feet dangle to the floor. "And what is her cause?"

Yvette shrugged and shimmied out of her trousers. "Power of some sort. I'm not certain of specifics. I only know she has been hoarding money and trying to bring teachers and students under her control." Now stark naked, she wandered over to her washstand, grabbed a towel, and began to dry herself.

Quit staring, Catalina. It's nothing you haven't seen before.

But after that kiss…

Lina nearly forgot herself in the memory of that kiss. She'd been completely swept away by the aching sweetness of it. Yvette had poured herself into the kiss: her eagerness and curiosity, her iron will and her gentle heart. If that kiss had been a book, Lina would know all there was to know about her. Sadly, Lina was not fluent in le baiser d'Yvette.

Or maybe not so sadly.

I will simply have to keep kissing her until I learn everything.

"Von Arx made deals with my father, the original Redbeard," Yvette continued. "She used her students to build the machines he used in his pillaging. Most of them had no idea what the machines were made for. He also recruited girls from the school, like Brigid. He wanted them on his crew for their knowledge of engineering and languages, and for their social polish. They could sneak into places the girls he'd recruited off the streets could not." She stepped into a clean pair of trousers and yanked them up. "Of course he didn't bother to send me to school, even though I'm his only natural daughter."

"That's why you took up his name." Lina nodded her understanding. Nasty father. Definitely a piece of why Yvette was both hard and vulnerable.

For best results, try conversation plus kissing.

"The name gives me status and connections. I've taken his smuggling routes and made deals with all the best of his contacts. But we do not destroy or murder or some of the other terrible things he did. We want to live free, not to claim the world as our own. So there is a void left by my father's death. Headmistress von Arx may desire to take that position for herself. I am not certain."

"And some people want to join her and some do not, which is why the school is falling apart and the girls are in danger?" Lina guessed.

Yvette buttoned up her new shirt. "Oui. As far as I know. I know nothing of her true plans. Now do you understand?"

"I do. Thank you."

"Good." Yvette returned to her closet, where she selected a green lace-up vest to complete her outfit. Apparently she never wore a corset. With her small breasts, she could probably do without undergarments at most times.

Lina smiled. That would prove useful when they decided to go beyond kissing. She waited for Yvette to finish dressing, then said, "Perhaps while we are here, we should talk about what happened in the bath."

Yvette sank into her reading chair. She gave Lina a wry grin. "I thought that was what you wanted when you summoned me here. There are no rules and you want more."

"Yes." No sense in denying it. "We clearly possess a strong physical attraction, and I see no reason not to act on it like free, rational adults."

Lina let herself bask in the feeling of normalcy. No overly-romantic daydreams. Simply a sensible arrangement for mutual enjoyment. This would be the perfect way to bring some relaxation to her time on the ship. And she was certain Yvette needed the release as much as she did.

"Good," Yvette declared. "It has been a long time for me. I have been busy pirating, and sometimes I am jealous of Esme and Kaina."

"They are lovers?" There was so much Lina still didn't know about the crew.

"They are matelots."

Lina's nose wrinkled. "I don't know that word."

"Matelotage is like a pirate marriage," Yvette explained. "Matelots share their earnings and pledge to protect and care for one another. If one gets hurt, the other will provide for them. If one dies, the other will inherit. It can be done between friends, but is often between lovers."

"A very sensible arrangement."

Lina approved. In a hazardous profession such as pirating, a formal arrangement for the security of oneself and one's partners was wise. In fact, a written agreement for any relationship was a good way to ensure all participants had a shared understanding of the situation and boundaries.

"Perhaps we should write down the basic parameters for our intimate relationship," she suggested. Her gaze darted around the room. "Do you have pen and paper?"

"Er…" Yvette shifted in her chair, crossing and uncrossing her legs.

"Oh, I don't wish to imply that I'm looking for anything as permanent as a matelotage," Lina added quickly. This was why communication was vital. She'd unsettled Yvette already with vague wording. "I've never been a romantic."

Never?

Lina shook off the twinge of conscience. A youthful fantasy was different than rational adult behavior.

"But I do enjoy casual companionship," she finished.

Yvette gave an awkward laugh. "Of course." She opened

the desk drawer, rose from her seat, and gestured for Lina to take her place.

"Thank you."

Lina found paper, pen, and ink, and arranged them all neatly on the desk before taking a seat. She tested the pen discreetly in the corner of the paper, then wrote in precise strokes at the top of the page, "Agreement Re: Physical Intimacies."

Yvette leaned against the wall beside the desk, staring down at the paper with a bemused expression.

"To avoid any misunderstandings, here is what I propose." Lina held her pen poised as she addressed the other woman. "Item one: nothing we do should interfere with your duties or mine."

Yvette looked affronted. "Certainly not! I would not do such a thing."

"I thought not." Lina committed the rule to paper. "Item two: I believe any physical affection or intimacies should be reserved for when we are in private. This will help to reinforce item one."

When Yvette voiced no objection, Lina wrote down the rule. With every stroke of the pen, she breathed easier. This was the right course of action. She could set parameters and corral her desires into a safe, comfortable space. Yes, she was aboard a pirate ship, but she wouldn't succumb to lawlessness.

She glanced up at Yvette's soft pink lips. Lina *would* allow herself to succumb to temptation, but only in a mature, controlled fashion.

"Item three," she continued. "This item is non-negotiable for me, though I cannot imagine you would object. Each encounter is to be taken on its own, with no guarantees that any particular act or behavior from a previous encounter is permissible."

Yvette nodded.

"And similarly for item four: both parties reserve the right to change their mind or call a halt at any time during the proceedings."

Yvette's mouth ticked up at the corners. "You are very…"

"Organized?" Lina suggested.

"Judicial." She waved a hand. "Continue."

"Yes, well…" Lina tried not to frown. Was 'judicial' a compliment, an insult, or merely an observation? She put the matter aside and forged ahead. "Item five: specifics such as location, duration, and so forth can be mutually agreed upon as need arises. Six: there will be no obligation or expectation to continue the relationship beyond the term of my employment on this vessel. Seven: earlier termination can be initiated by either party." She paused in her writing. "Though I can't imagine we would tire of one another so quickly, can you?"

Yvette had gone oddly still. Her blue eyes focused on Lina with rapier-sharp intensity. "You are a curious woman," she said softly. "Like a mysterious old map that compels you to follow it."

That was definitely a compliment. Lina arched her eyebrows and gave Yvette a seductive grin. "Follow it all the way to my treasure trove."

The words did not have the desired effect. Yvette laughed. "You Americans have very silly words for these things. French is better."

"I'd be happy for you to give me lessons," Lina purred. "Do you have additional terms to add, or do we have an agreement?"

Yvette considered for a moment, twisting a strand of hair around her finger. "Oui. I accept."

Lina signed her name at the bottom of the paper with a flourish, then handed the pen to her soon-to-be lover. Yvette's impulsive kiss in the bath had been magnificent. But this would be even better.

14

YVETTE GAVE HER EGG a gentle tap, opening a narrow crack at the top. Using her small spoon, she gently pried away the shell, revealing the layer of springy white that hid the gooey yolk inside. Her usual breakfast. One egg, in a delicate cup, consumed in a ladylike manner.

Plus an insulated flask filled with black coffee.

All around her, the pirates chatted, excited for their arrival today. Several of them were excited to see Amira, a former Daughter of Redbeard who now oversaw the Haven in Algiers. All of them were excited for the opportunity to relax for a day, enjoying the beauty of the Mediterranean coast.

Yvette's mind, as usual, kept drifting away from the conversation. All it could focus on this morning was Lina. Lina and her perfect hair and clothing. Lina and her precisely arranged breakfast tray. Lina and her sex contract.

Yvette reached absently for the salt, knocking the shaker onto its side. A few tiny grains bounced across the table. She hurriedly righted it and liberally sprinkled her egg. No one had noticed her clumsiness, had they? Or if they had, they wouldn't know the reason, non?

Lina gave her a sly smile. A smile that said, "*I* know the reason." She'd been sending smiles like that across the table from the moment Yvette had sat down.

Wasn't that against the contract? Lina had specified that the affair was to be conducted in private. Or had that not included flirting? Did they need to add a provision about flirting?

Perhaps Lina didn't consider flirtations to be anything special. She probably flirted like this all the time with all the ladies.

Yvette stared down at her egg, which she had mauled in a decidedly non-ladylike manner.

Merde.

While Lina took proper, delicate bites, Yvette scarfed down the rest of her breakfast like the pirate she was, then trudged topside—with her coffee—to prepare for landing.

Algiers looked exactly as Yvette remembered from her one prior visit: sparkling water, a steady stream of airships and watercraft, and building after building rising up the rolling hills. As La Liberté settled to the ground, the people came into clear view, their varied modes of dress a colorful tribute to the cosmopolitan nature of the port city.

Workers on the ground tossed mooring ropes up to the crew, who secured the ship while Yvette shut down the engine. A clear day, a smooth landing, and a completed task. Another hour or two, and she could take a break from her captain's duties. And perhaps find some time with Lina to relieve the urges that had been pestering her all morning.

One-by-one, the crew finished their tasks and gathered on the deck. With their smiling faces and their dashing uniforms, they looked like conquering heroes returning to an adoring populace. Pride surged through Yvette. These ladies were indeed heroes, to one another and to all women who sought to seize their own happiness. Maybe she wasn't a perfect captain, but her crew was as fine as she could want.

She strode to the rail, the tails of her coat fanning out behind her. The dark red velvet with its elaborate gold embroidery and gleaming buttons was perhaps a trifle ostentatious, but Yvette wanted to be highly visible today. Amira needed to be able to spot her from the ground. Besides, what was the point of being a pirate captain if you didn't have at least one fabulous coat?

Yvette raised a hand to shield her eyes and scanned the ground below. Curse that sewer for stealing her hat! Perhaps she could find a new one in the market here. Mediterranean pirates needed to buy their clothing somewhere.

"What if I don't want to leave the ship?" one of the girls asked from behind Yvette.

"I'm sure arrangements can be made," Lina reassured her. "We will never leave the ship entirely unattended. But if you do choose to disembark it doesn't mean you must remain here. It's a beautiful day, and you may wish to enjoy the seaside with your friends before you make a final decision."

"That does sound pleasant," the girl conceded. "As long as you're sure…"

"I will personally push aside anyone impeding your path back to the ship," Lina promised.

She was so good at her job. One of the most remarkably competent people Yvette had ever met. Fortune must have worn a dazzling smile the day Lina had set foot aboard this ship.

A flash of emerald green in the corner of her vision pulled Yvette back to her intended task. Not Amira, but that was her favored color. Yvette's gaze hopped from green point to green point, finally locating her contact among a crowd of people greeting arrivals. Success! She lifted a hand and waved.

Amira waved back with both hands, a strangely expressive gesture for someone intending to go unnoticed in the throng. Perhaps she thought Yvette couldn't find her? Yvette waved again, trying to meet Amira's gaze despite the distance.

Wheels crunched on gravel, announcing the arrival of the roll-away staircase. Yvette glanced down. A pair of burly men pushed the apparatus toward La Liberté, their approach not quite perpendicular to the ship's rail. Newbies. The more experienced ground crews knew it was easier to align the stairs first rather than at the end.

A hand touched Yvette's shoulder and she jumped.

"Is that woman in the green our contact?" Lina asked. Her fingers rubbed back and forth for a second before dropping away. Perhaps enjoying the texture of the velvet. Perhaps not.

"Oui. Why do—"

Yvette knew the answer the moment she lifted her head. Amira's waves had become larger now, almost frantic. She made a slashing gesture across her throat.

Yvette cursed. That could mean only two things: you're dead, or kill the mission. Or maybe both.

"Back away from the rail!" she ordered. "We have a problem." She began to shrug out of her coat. "I will go speak to Amira and report back."

The staircase bumped against the hull at approximately a forty-five degree angle. Yvette swung a leg over the rail. To the devil with proper safety protocol. She needed to speak to Amira now.

A metallic buzzing stopped her before she could step across the gap. A silver projectile a few centimeters long popped out of the hollow end of one of the handrails, landing on the deck with a clink. Several more followed. Then dozens, sailing past Yvette to skitter across the ship, their pointy snouts digging into the woodwork.

"Termites!" Esme shouted.

Yvette kicked at the staircase, trying to angle it away from the ship, but the two men below held it fast. Bastards! Bracing herself with her left hand on the rail, she yanked one of her antique flintlocks from the holster at her hip and fired at the closest of the men. They ran.

"They're drilling into the ship!"

Yvette kicked at the staircase again, but it barely moved. She'd never stop the flow of bugs this way.

"Spread out!" Lina commanded behind her. "Stomp them! Guard the machinery!"

Yvette swung around, dropping back to the deck to find hundreds of the drill-nosed creatures scrambling in all directions.

Lina slammed her foot down on one of the termites. When she lifted her boot, the tiny machine lay helpless on the deck, its drill still spinning, but its body crushed and immobile. A few drops of glowing green luxene oozed from the tangled metal.

"Stomp them!" she shouted again. "Their bodies are fragile!"

"Allez!" Yvette ordered. "Go!" She raced to Lina's side, pulverizing every termite she could reach. "You are commanding my crew now?"

Lina bent to pry a termite out of a plank and flung it overboard. "You were busy."

Yvette ground her heel into a bug that had crawled much too close to her discarded coat. "Do not damage that," she growled, and yanked the coat off the deck. Slinging the coat around her shoulders, she ran for the bridge. Dozens of the remaining insects crawled up the half-flight of stairs, heading for the sensitive navigation equipment.

Lina followed. She hopped up the stairs, trampling bugs as she went. "What did you expect me to do? Nothing?"

"Non." Yvette lunged for the controls, prepping for takeoff and starting up the engines. Thank goodness the boilers hadn't had a chance to cool down yet. "Zahra! Release the ropes!"

Yvette moved through the steps without conscious thought. Her gaze swept over the gauges, but her mind registered none of the numbers. Everything was automatic. The way she'd done it a thousand times before.

Thank God her body knew what it was doing, because she couldn't tear her focus off of Lina, who danced around her, smashing termites. One of the little monsters crawled up the side of the control panel. Yvette flicked it away and Lina ground it to bits beneath her toe.

"You are an excellent pirate," Yvette praised her.

Lina froze. "Who, me?" She shook her head and went right back to her task.

"Yes."

The ship began to rise into the air. Thank you, Zahra. Yvette turned her eyes to the sky in front of her, but her ears remained attuned to Lina.

"You don't panic in a crisis," Yvette explained. "You look out for the rest of the crew. You know when to break the rules. You were smart to take charge and give orders."

"Hold still, there's one between your feet."

Lina grasped Yvette's waist and slid a leg between hers to dispose of the termite. The contact lasted only a second, but the friction of thigh rubbing against thigh sent waves of heat pulsing through her entire body.

No, no, no. This was not the time.

Her fingers tightened on the wheel, easing La Liberté into a slow turn. Wind tugged at her hair, the familiar sensation coaxing her to sink into the oblivion of flying.

"Got you, you slippery bastard!" Lina declared. "That's the last one. I'm heading down to help the others. Shout if you need me."

Yvette blew out a slow breath, but her muscles remained clenched. Yes, she needed Lina. Needed her body to relieve this incessant lust. Needed her wit and wisdom to support the crew and help solve problems.

But needing was dangerous. Today's attack had been premeditated. Which meant an enemy had known where they were going. Information that had been restricted to her most trusted allies.

Betrayal.

Yvette's stomach churned. She kicked at the battered carcass of a mechanical termite. Today was a good reminder of why she always kept herself at a distance from the crew. And why she needed to keep a distance from Lina too.

Captain Redbeard could only depend on herself. Herself, her ship, and the air currents. Always adrift. Never attached.

15

WHY WAS SHE HERE?

Lina lowered herself into a seat at the dining table, directly across from Yvette. Silence draped the room like a shroud. Only a short time ago, this space had echoed with laughter and merry conversation. Now seats sat empty but for a few somber faces.

Why was she here?

Yvette had called an emergency meeting with her top advisors: first mate Zahra and purser Kaina. And Lina. As if she were a vital part of the crew and not a greenhorn who'd served only a handful of days.

Yvette pushed a tangled lock of hair out of her face. Her windblown tresses were the only overt sign of the chaos of their failed landing. Her face was calm, her eyes ice hard. The overhead lamps highlighted the intricate gold swirls embroidered on the lapels of her long coat. Perfectly tailored and of the finest velvet, the garment proclaimed her rank and power. This was Captain Redbeard. Cold. Hard. Determined.

"You know we have a problem," Yvette stated, her voice as icy as her persona. "We have an enemy, and they know our plans. This is possible in only two ways. Either they can read our coded messages, or someone on this ship has betrayed us."

"None of the crew would do such a thing," Kaina vowed. "I am certain of it."

Zahra folded her hands in her lap. "I wouldn't say it was impossible. But very, very unlikely. I would trust any of these women with my life."

Both the women had full confidence in their statements, as far as Lina could tell. No tics in the face or hands. No unusual shifting. Neither too much nor too little eye contact.

And she agreed with them. The crew had demonstrated nothing but loyalty and friendship during her time here. If there was a liar anywhere among them, she was exceptional.

"I hope you are both correct," Yvette replied. She'd hardly moved since Lina had sat down. Her back remained straight and her hands rested atop the table, unnaturally still. No shifting. No fidgeting.

This Captain Redbeard was a complete fabrication. Yvette's full attention had gone into presenting an aura of control. Good for ensuring that the ship ran smoothly. But surely bad for the real woman beneath.

"I have already given our new course to the team on flight duty," Yvette continued. "We will fly to visit La Capitaine in England to consult about the code machine and make arrangements for the girls from the Institute. Further decisions will be made afterward."

Lina nodded and gave Yvette a small smile. Excellent phrasing. No one was specifically excluded from the future decisions. Yet.

"Any questions?"

Zahra and Kaina shook their heads.

"The plan is good," Kaina agreed.

Zahra pushed her chair back from the table. "I will inform the crew."

Yvette stood, her every movement slow and deliberate. "Thank you. You may tell the crew they can come to me with any concerns." Her brows narrowed. "Or confessions."

Lina's gaze settled on Yvette's hands, willing her to twitch. A tap of a finger against her thigh would do. She could rub the soft velvet of her coat. Or play with the shiny buttons. Anything to reveal her true self, the part that was soft and sweet—and undoubtedly hurting.

Kaina and Zahra started for the door, and Lina scrambled to her feet, suddenly aware of her complete lack of participation in the conversation. She'd been nothing but an observer. An outsider. Why the hell had Yvette wanted her here?

"Catalina, a word," the captain murmured.

Lina froze. Perhaps her question was about to be answered. "Yes?"

Yvette clasped her hands behind her back. "I know you are not leaking information to the enemy. You were not here before the first attack, and you had no knowledge of our likely enemies. I can trust you in this matter."

Trust based on concrete proof of innocence wasn't really trust at all, but Lina didn't argue the point, much as she wanted to. She needed to hear everything Yvette had to say.

"You also understand people," Yvette went on. "I don't like the idea that any of these women would betray us. I want to believe them all. But I will also suspect them all. That isn't helpful, is it?"

"Not particularly, no. But entirely natural. You've been hurt, and you don't know who did it. Withdrawing from your friends is one way to protect yourself. Denying the truth is another."

A calculated smile touched Yvette's lips. "A good demonstration of your talents. This is how you can help. You will be able to tell if anyone is acting strangely. I need you to pay attention and report anything unusual to me. We can have regular meetings."

Lina folded her arms across her chest. "Don't you think private meetings will have a negative effect on morale? The others will think we're up to something."

Yvette's brow furrowed—her first spontaneous reaction since Lina had entered the room. "Why would they care? I told you, there are no rules about shipboard relations. You wrote a contract."

Lina's pulse leapt. Yvette was still thinking about her. About their agreement and what they might get up to in bed.

Blast it all. What a time to be distracted by prurient thoughts.

"I meant they might think we were conspiring," Lina explained, hoping a return to the original topic would stem the flow of lurid images through her mind. "They will think I'm spying for you. I can't do that. If it becomes us against them, it will undermine your authority as captain. And I can't break the trust of my clients. If they can't confide in me, I can't do my job."

Yvette met Lina's gaze with an icy stare. "My duty is to protect the crew. If there is a leak, it must be found before anyone else is hurt. I cannot spare their feelings at the cost of lives. I *must* know if anyone poses a danger to the others. And feelings are fleeting things." She spread her hands and shrugged in a particularly French manner.

Lina cocked her head and frowned down at Yvette. "You don't really believe that."

Yvette stared stonily back.

"I know you don't believe it because I know you have feelings lingering deep inside. Some that go back a long time. I've spied traces now and then." She took a step closer and lowered her voice. "And I know this possible betrayal hurts you now."

"I am very well, thank you." Yvette waved a hand. "You may leave now. Report to me if you see anything suspicious."

"Yvette." Lina closed the remaining distance between them. "You don't have to pretend with me." She risked a gentle touch to Yvette's arm. Lord, how she wanted to crack through that shell and release the woman she thought she'd begun to know.

Yvette flinched at the contact, but didn't pull away. Had her icy gaze begun to soften at last?

"Why be the captain with a heart of steel," Lina whispered, "when you can be Yvette with a heart of fire? She's the woman who entices me. The woman I would like to see for 'regular meetings.'" She dipped her chin, offering a kiss. "We could begin right now."

Yvette's warm breath ghosted over Lina's lips. "Are you trying to distract me from my purpose?" A huskiness had crept into her voice. She needed this, as much or more than Lina did.

"No. I'm trying to be rational."

This didn't feel rational. It felt impulsive and risky, but that was likely an aftereffect of the misadventure with the mechanical termites. Her body had yet to settle.

"Our urges are particularly strong after a brush with danger," Lina explained. Perhaps not strictly true, at least on her side. Her craving for Yvette had been steadily increasing since the moment they'd met. "Engaging in intercourse to relieve the tension is entirely logical. Orgasm is an excellent stress relief and relaxation technique. It's a scientific fact."

"And you have… studied this?" Yvette bit her bottom lip.

Scorching desire surged through Lina. Yvette's slightly crooked teeth pressed into the soft, pink bow of her lip. God, she was just begging for a nibble, a lick, a deep, drugging taste.

"Extensively," Lina purred. "Shall I show you?"

Yvette hesitated, her lip reddening where her teeth still worried at the plump flesh.

Lina's spirits dropped with every second that passed. This wasn't going to happen. Not now. Which meant maybe not ever.

An ache began to build in her chest.

Yvette took a step backward.

Dammit.

Lina opened her mouth to speak, but before any words could form, Yvette extended her hand.

"My cabin or yours?" she asked.

Lina's heart leapt for joy. No, not joy. Surely that was too extreme a term. Excitement. Her heart was pounding with excitement.

She entwined her fingers with Yvette's. "Yours."

"Good." Yvette gave a brusque nod. "Mine has a much nicer bed."

16

YVETTE LOCKED THE DOOR to her cabin, then began shedding clothes. Since she cared little for any of it besides her coat, most of the items ended up in a pile on the floor. Boots, trousers, vest…

She had gotten nearly half her shirt buttons undone, when a chuckle from Lina made her pause.

"Eager to get started?" Lina's suspenders were dangling, and her shirtwaist was unbuttoned to expose the corset underneath. A pastel pink corset. With tiny flowers embroidered all over it in glittering silver thread. Silver and pink satin ribbons had been woven together to decorate the top edge of the garment. Tiny pink bows, also satin, hid the clasps down the center.

It was not a corset for practical, scientifically-proven stress relief.

It wasn't practical at all, in Yvette's opinion, with all those frivolous bits and pieces that could poke or scratch, or leave bumps beneath one's shirt.

Except for seduction. It was highly practical for seduction, offering up Lina's breasts in a tantalizing manner. Yvette had the urge to run a finger along those soft swells. Perhaps followed by her tongue. But that didn't seem fitting for a pragmatic tryst, either.

She went back to work on her shirt buttons. "Don't you want me naked?"

Not everyone did. Some men had preferred to grope her through her clothes and lift her skirts. Back when she'd actually worn skirts. The one other woman she'd been with had liked Yvette to lounge naked on the bed or a couch, but had rarely removed much of her own clothing. Yvette went along with whatever her lovers preferred. Unfortunately, she had absolutely no idea what Lina preferred.

"Of course I do." Lina's wicked smile sent shivers down Yvette's spine. "But don't rush on my account. Which suits you today? Get right to business or take it slow?"

Yvette looked down at the last of her buttons to hide her confusion. Why was Lina asking that question? Surely there was only one sensible answer. They had other concerns. They weren't storybook lovers with nothing better to do than while away the hours basking in a haze of perpetual infatuation. Like lying in a meadow, gazing longingly into one another's eyes. Or snuggled in bed, feeding one another bonbons and reciting love poetry. Honestly, how silly was that?

She snorted.

"Did I say something funny?"

Yvette glanced up. Lina's dark eyes were locked on her face, studying her with open curiosity.

"My brain went drifting off," Yvette admitted. "It does that."

She tossed her shirt aside, leaving her in only her small cotton knickers and silk stockings. Despite this, Lina's attention remained on her face.

Yvette stifled a sigh. She wasn't much to look at, she supposed. Her figure was boyish, all muscle and bone, sharp and angular. She lacked the softness of a pretty woman like Lina.

Which was fine. She was a pirate captain, and pirates weren't soft.

Lina shimmied out of her split skirt. "You're an intriguing woman."

Intriguing. That was good.

I am a fierce, intriguing pirate.

Yvette yanked off the last of her underthings and climbed into the bed. "I'm ready."

It was time to get this over with. She was stressed, she was lustful, and she needed something to focus on before she started inserting Lina into the bonbon-eating scenario. Lina in her damned frilly corset, her lips covered with chocolate.

Lina wasn't slow to undress, but she was neat and orderly about it, and she had more layers to remove. Yvette's uncertainty grew with every second that passed. Would this really help? Did Lina really want her? Would that bonbon fantasy ever disappear from her head?

"So." The bed shifted as Lina stretched out beside Yvette. "Tell me what you'd like."

"Whatever pleases you," Yvette replied automatically. It was the safest course. She liked knowing her lovers would find the experience satisfying.

Now that this was happening, she was free to admire Lina in a way she hadn't allowed herself before. Her lips were marvelous; slim and delicate, but rosy and with a gloriously enticing curve and a deep dip at the top of the bow. Her dark brown eyes were a fathomless secret, framed by enviously long, dark lashes. And below that lovely face lay an expanse of perfect skin, a warm, dark cream with olive undertones.

"I already know what pleases me," Lina replied. "I'd like to know what would please *you.*"

"Oh, anything." Whatever Lina wanted, Yvette would do it. She wouldn't be the girl that disappointed someone. "Pleasing you pleases me."

Lina waited silently, her beautiful eyes fixed on Yvette's face.

Yvette squirmed, willing Lina to simply say something.

She'd seemed to like it when Yvette had planted that impulsive kiss on her in the bath, so maybe she wanted Yvette to touch her first. Why not simply say so? Yvette would be perfectly happy to run her hands up and down Lina's long legs. Or pinch her perky red-brown nipples.

"Hmm," Lina murmured.

What did that mean? When Lina had made this offer, Yvette had imagined a quick coupling, a "thank you, that was nice," and a return to business. They still had cleanup and repairs from the termite mess. Yet here was Lina, asking questions and acting mysterious.

Lina traced one finger along Yvette's collarbone, sending a rush of arousal straight to her groin. The breath whooshed out of her lungs. She'd had no idea she'd be so sensitive there. Or was it only Lina's touch that made the area so erotic? She did say she'd had plenty of experience.

"Stop me if you don't like something," Lina said, trailing her finger downward to brush along the very edge of Yvette's left breast.

Yvette's pulse began to quicken. Lina's leisurely movements were the exact opposite of everything she had expected. And already she couldn't remember why that was. Why would she want anything else?

Lina's fingers continued their exploration, mapping Yvette's torso with light, fleeting touches. Every time Yvette gasped or flinched, the corners of Lina's mouth quirked upward. She was a treasure hunter, honing in on the best places to dig.

Yvette tipped over onto her back, and Lina straddled her, thighs clamping around hips as she rocked their pelvises together.

Yvette made a noise somewhere between an "ooh" and an "ah." She'd meant to say "oui" or "yes" or "more," but words wouldn't form.

"Do you like that?"

Lina rocked her hips, creating just enough friction to draw

another noise from Yvette's throat. Mon Dieu, she was sensitive today. Was it the stress? The prolonged period of abstinence? Some secret sex magic that only Lina knew about?

"How about this?" Lina cupped her hands around Yvette's breasts, kneading gently.

Yvette managed a nod. Yes. Absolutely. Lina's hands were a perfect fit, exactly the right size to fondle and squeeze without making Yvette feel small or inadequate. In fact, the pink flush creeping over Lina's chest and the tautness of her nipples made Yvette feel the opposite of inadequate. She aroused Lina. Without even touching her.

When Lina thumbed Yvette's nipples, Yvette had to return the favor. It was imperative. She simply couldn't stop her hands from moving across Lina's chest and giving playful little pinches to those dusky tips.

"Harder," Lina urged.

Yvette increased the pressure.

A glazed look entered Lina's eyes. "Mmm. Yes. Like that." She arched into Yvette's touch. "You are so, so lovely. Tell me what you want next. Or show me, if speaking is too much."

The ache between Yvette's legs grew more insistent with every second Lina touched her. She wriggled her hips, in the hopes that would say enough. What else could she do? She didn't want to take her hands off Lina's body. Lina was so soft and warm and she stared at Yvette with such unabashed desire.

Lina slid partially off Yvette, wedging her knee between Yvette's legs to nudge them apart. Her hands inched down Yvette's body, leaving a scorching trail of sensation so intense, Yvette thought she might explode when Lina reached her core.

But, no. It was worse. And so much better.

Lina's fingers feathered over the tight blond curls protecting Yvette's sex, then eased between her legs. The caress was smooth and light, almost tender, in a way Yvette had never experienced. The tension inside her ratcheted higher, higher.

"So soft," Lina murmured. "So wet for me."

Yvette could hardly breathe. She'd forgotten what to do with her hands or the rest of her body. How had she not broken yet? She was an overheated boiler, an overinflated balloon. Lina was going to turn la petit mort into literal death.

"You like gentle, don't you?" Lina's voice had grown throatier, almost breathless, as if she were getting off on this as well.

Yvette moaned as Lina's finger teased her clit with that same maddening lightness. Gentle made no sense. She was hard and rough and piratical, and, oh, God, oh, God, this was torture. Perfect, blissful torture.

A hand caught hers, guiding it to where Lina was equally wet and eager.

"Touch me. Yes, like..." Her words morphed into an extended sigh. "That."

Release. She needs release. I need it. We need it.

Lina thrust against Yvette's hand, begging for more. As Yvette stroked Lina's clit in firmer, faster circles, Lina did the same in return, driving all thought from Yvette's mind except this desperate need for them both to climax.

Closer. Closer. Please, please, pl—

Yvette screamed. Her back arched, lifting her hips clear off the bed. Half-atop her, Lina whimpered and trembled, riding out a long climax before finally nudging Yvette's hand away.

Time seemed to hold still as they lay there, in a tangled heap, panting and shaken. It felt right, this closeness. Comfortable. Uncomplicated. Lina's hair had come loose from its bun and now splayed across the sheets and over her shoulders. She fit here, among the rumpled bedding and the mingled scents of sex and perfumed soap.

Lina stretched her arms above her head and broke the silence. "Well, if all our meetings are like this, we will have to make them a highly regular occurrence. There are many, many things I'd like to do with you."

Yvette shifted toward the edge of the bed.

Regular meetings. The contract.

This was a tryst. A fling. Lina would leave someday. This was stress relief and a bit of fun, and that was all it ever could be.

Yvette pushed herself out of bed and began to gather up her clothing, turning herself back into Captain Redbeard. And pretending her legs weren't still wobbly—and her heart a little melted—from the best orgasm of her life.

17

"And I know Olga is safe with the doctor and we'll pick her up as soon as we can, but…" Angelique slumped in the plush chair where Lina's clients usually sat. She twisted one long braid around her finger. Furrows of worry on her ebony skin spoke of the depth of her concern as much as the hitch in her voice did.

"Take your time," Lina said. "I'm listening."

This was the first time Angelique had visited Lina. The first time they'd talked at all, in fact. Angelique was soft-spoken and liked to keep busy. Her role was a scientific one Lina didn't yet grasp. Something with charts and measurements and discussions of aerodynamics.

Angelique composed herself. "We've never been apart this long," she admitted. "Not since we were seven or eight years old. All the women in the organization called each other 'Sister,' but between Olga and I it was true. We are family."

Lina nodded. "Sometimes ties of friendship are the strongest bonds in a person's life. Family doesn't need to be blood. I can't take your loneliness and worry away, but I can tell you that these feelings are valid and show how much you care."

Angelique smiled and hopped up from her seat. "Merci.

The others were right. It's good to speak my troubles aloud. I should return to work."

Lina hurried to stand. "I'll be here any time you need to talk. And you know about my more comprehensive services, should you ever need them."

"Where you ask questions until we spill the secrets of our whole life?" Angelique's brows arched mischievously. "Clara has told us all about it." She sobered. "May I ask *you* a question?"

"Of course."

"Why are you avoiding the captain today?"

Lina blinked twice, then frowned. "What?"

"The captain is grumpy. You weren't sitting with her at breakfast. I haven't seen you talk to her once, when usually you are together often."

"Yvette is focused on our upcoming landing, and I've had a number of clients. Nothing unusual."

"The crew was worried the two of you had an argument. I'm glad we were wrong." Angelique headed for the door with a wave of farewell.

Lina sank back into her chair, rubbing her temple. The crew thought she and Yvette were arguing? Because they hadn't sat together at breakfast?

Someone had probably heard their tryst yesterday. They hadn't been particularly quiet. Perhaps a romantically-minded crew member had made conjectures and started a rumor. Anyone expecting cuddles and poetry could easily misconstrue a sensible arrangement.

And Lina had behaved in a perfectly sensible manner. Scouring the ship for termite damage was a full-crew endeavor, on top of their usual duties. The extra burden fell especially hard on Yvette. Lina didn't want to disrupt that, even for delightfully good sex. Item one of the contract explicitly stated that the affair was not to interfere with anything else. She would absolutely not be sidling up to Yvette to kiss her good morning like a besotted wife.

But you want to, don't you? Just like you wanted to cuddle her yesterday and ask her to spend the whole night with you.

"Do you need to move into the client chair?" Lina asked herself out loud. God, she hated it when her brain tried to turn analytical on herself. It made her insides squirm.

And why is that?

"Stop it." She shot to her feet and stomped up top to watch the ship land.

The weather today was sunny, with a light breeze, and La Liberté glided easily down into the English countryside. Yvette lowered the ship onto a wide field of grass, beside the most enormous house Lina had ever seen.

Mansions were nothing new to her. Savannah was full of large, glamorous houses. But Savannah was still a city, with limited space. This ducal manor sprawled across the field, four stories tall and easily three times as wide as an upper-class Savannah home.

"I'd heard Sabine was a duchess now, but I didn't realize she lived in an actual palace," Lina murmured.

"You know Sabine?"

Lina jumped at the sound of Yvette's voice. Her pulse began to race and her muscles tensed. This was a classic three-Fs reaction. She obviously didn't want to fight Yvette. Which left her body preparing to either flee or fuck. The latter. It had to be. Fleeing would be silly, and yesterday's assignation had been spectacular. It was natural to crave more.

"I, uh…" Lina took a step backward. "Yes. I met Sabine when she was Nora's patient. It was a number of years ago, but she's not the sort of woman one forgets."

A fond smile rose to Lina's lips. Sabine was exactly the sort of woman she liked. Capable, loyal, smart, and a bit dangerous. Lina might have tried to seduce her, if Sabine hadn't preferred men. Instead, they'd become friends.

"Ah."

The word came out almost as a huff, and Lina raised a questioning eyebrow as her gaze refocused on Yvette.

"That will save introductions," the captain continued in her no-nonsense tone. "You and I will go speak with her."

"Why me?"

Yvette lowered her voice. "Because you are not a spy."

Of course. She was "trusted." A rush of anger heated Lina's skin. Couldn't Yvette trust her for her integrity, rather than by default? Especially after what they'd shared yesterday?

Sex doesn't have to result in closeness, Lina, you know that!

"I'm not a spy," she agreed, the words perhaps a bit too brusque. At least Yvette trusted Lina with her body. That was a start. And it wasn't as if she trusted anyone else, either. Being angry about it was irrational.

"The rest of the crew will remain with the ship," Yvette informed Lina. "They are to keep watch and be prepared to flee at any moment. I will not have a repeat of the termite incident." She waved a hand at the rope ladder dangling over the rail. "Let's go."

Yvette led the way down, then strode off toward the mansion, the tails of her coat fanning out to give tantalizing glimpses of her comely posterior. Lina trailed after in silence. The crew was right. Something was amiss. The deep relaxation she'd felt in the aftermath of sex had worn off entirely, leaving her at least as tense as she'd been before. Judging by Yvette's body language, she felt the same.

"Do we need to make our stress relief sessions a daily ritual?" Lina asked.

Yvette faltered. "Pardon?" she choked out.

"Sorry to startle you. It occurred to me that we didn't discuss the matter yesterday. I know we could both benefit from more release."

Yvette's steps slowed, and she turned her head to frown at

Lina. The expression made her bottom lip plump out enticingly. "Why do you ask me this now?"

"Because…" Lina snapped her mouth closed. Oh, hell. She *had* been avoiding Yvette. Why now? The question had only one truthful answer.

Because I want you now. Because every second I'm near you I crave you more.

Some part of her must have known and counseled her to stay away. She could dismiss last night's desires as mere post-coital euphoria. But Yvette had been infiltrating her mind all day. Her lips. Her hands. The way she surrendered to Lina's touch.

Now they were side-by-side, and Lina itched for more. A taste. A caress. And another and another.

Damn and blast. This was not the time. No wonder her subconscious had sought distance. Lina could control her body, but not her thoughts. She couldn't stop the wanting any more than she could stop the earth's rotation.

"There's Sabine." Yvette made an abrupt gesture. "We can talk about other things later."

Lina's gaze turned toward the gardens. The pirate-turned-duchess danced through a maze of greenery, silver sword flashing in the sunlight. Her every movement was smooth and strong, despite a protruding belly that suggested an advanced stage of pregnancy. A little girl in a military-style jacket stood nearby, watching attentively and clutching her own wooden sword.

Sabine caught sight of Lina and Yvette approaching, but continued her demonstration without pause. The girl mimicked some of her motions.

"And that…" Sabine made a final lunge. "Is how the entire pattern will look when you've learned it. You want to be able to do it without thinking, so your arms and legs know all the movements when you have to face an opponent."

The girl nodded earnestly, then used her sword to point

toward Lina and Yvette. "Mommy, your pirate friends are here."

Sabine lifted her sword in greeting. "Hello." She nudged the girl. "Lola, why don't you run inside and find your father. We'll all gather for tea shortly, but first the ladies and I have some business to discuss."

Lola bounced up and down. "A secret pirate meeting?"

Yvette bent down and pressed a finger to her lips. "Very secret. Don't let the duke know. Tell him we're discussing new pirate fashions."

Lina's heart fluttered. Kindness to children. She would wager good money Yvette would coo at puppies, too. On the inside, the cool pirate captain was all softness. Curse whomever had hurt her enough that she'd built towering walls around herself.

The adults headed for the front doors at a leisurely pace, while Lola raced ahead.

"Nice coat," Sabine said to Yvette.

Yvette preened, stroking the red velvet. "It's my favorite."

"And Catalina, it's wonderful to see you! I didn't know you'd joined Redbeard's crew." Sabine gave her a delighted smile.

Lina smiled back. It was good to see Sabine healthy, happy, and thriving. Her past had been full of hardship, and she deserved peace and joy.

"A temporary assignment," Lina answered. "I'm pleased to be helping for a time."

Had it only been weeks since she'd left home? Somehow her old, orderly life seemed long ago and far away.

Sabine led the way into the house, to a spacious parlor with wide windows. She settled herself onto the largest available chair, sighing as she sank into the cushions. Lina and Yvette sat on the nearby sofa.

"I hope you don't mind my taking the best chair." Sabine patted her belly. "These two are currently engaging in fisticuffs."

"Twins?" Lina asked. "Congratulations."

"Thank you. Cliff is beside himself with excitement. I have to keep my sword with me to threaten him if he hovers too much. Now, about that peculiar message you sent me. You had questions about the Sphinx device?"

Yvette took over the conversation, explaining the recent attacks and her suspicions about their enemies. She finished by saying, "We need to know if anyone else might be able to break the codes the machine generates. Because if they can't, we have a leak."

"It's unbreakable, I'm afraid," Sabine replied. "We've consulted with mathematicians about it. If you have the device, or another identical one, and you know the settings, you can decipher the code. Without the machine, you would need a Babbage Analytical Engine—more powerful than any we've experimented with—to make the necessary calculations. Someone must be learning your plans in another way. I'm sorry."

Yvette's shoulders slumped, and she swore. "What about the girls?"

"We have plenty of room for them here," Sabine answered. "I'll find them safe places to go. Being a duchess is useful sometimes. And if necessary, I can fly them away myself."

"Thank you." Yvette squirmed in her seat, looking at the doorway as if she already wanted to leave.

"Do you have any more information about your enemies?" Sabine asked. "Who? Why?"

"Von Arx is involved. The bear-dragon looked like something the Institute would build. And then there were these." Yvette dug into her pocket and tossed something to Sabine.

The duchess held up the small metal object—a half-crushed mechanical termite. Her eyes widened and she fumbled the tiny machine, almost dropping it. "This is one of my termites!"

Yvette froze, her attention riveting on Sabine. "Yours?"

"I think so." Sabine adjusted her spectacles and peered carefully at the broken bug. "Yes. It's hard to see, the way it's squashed, but it does bear the Tagget Industries mark. This is the termite design I commissioned a few months ago."

Lina leaned forward in her seat. "You commissioned mechanical termites? I thought you were retired."

"Semi-retired," Sabine corrected. "My adoring public would be very sad if I were no longer the Pirate Duchess." She patted her belly again. "And I need to raise fierce children to carry on the legacy of the Mad Duke."

Yvette began to fidget once more, crossing her arms and drumming her fingers on her biceps. "Were these termites stolen from you?"

"Of course not." Sabine flicked the termite in the direction of a nearby writing desk, and it landed with a *ting* in a wastepaper bin. "All of mine are neatly stowed in a box aboard my ship. Someone else must have ordered their own."

Yvette pursed her lips. "I will contact this Tagget Industries and demand to know who purchased the termites."

"Perhaps a friendly telephone call?" Lina suggested.

The parlor door swung open, and a tall, dark-haired man wearing red spectacles swept into the room. He carried a large tray of tea and biscuits and stepped carefully, as if he feared he might trip and spill everything at any moment.

"Refreshments are here, ladies," he declared in a Midwestern American accent.

Lola popped into the room behind him. "I didn't tell him anything," she said proudly.

"Just the duke we need," Sabine declared.

The Duke of Hartleigh—a duke odd enough to serve his own tea could only be Sabine's husband—set the tray on the small table beside Sabine's chair and kissed her on the cheek. "What do you need me for, love?" He gave her a smoldering smile.

"Something you excel at." Sabine winked at him, then

poured a cup of tea. "Business telephone calls." She set three sugared biscuits on the saucer, then passed it to Yvette. "Catalina, would you like cream? Sugar? Biscuits?"

"None of the above, thank you."

The duke fetched a chair from the other side of the room and set it beside the tea table while Sabine finished passing out the tea.

"So," he asked, "who do you need me to call?"

"Tagget Industries. We need to know who else ordered mechanical termites." Yvette took a bite of biscuit, leaving a small streak of sugar on her lips.

Lina forced herself to look at the duke, who was holding his hands beneath the teapot while Lola poured. A good father and a kind man. Someone she would like to know, and entirely safe to look at. Not the least bit arousing.

"I'm afraid I can't... That's plenty, Lola. Thank you." He watched the girl set down the teapot, then sipped from his overfull cup. "I can't ask Tagget for that sort of information. Bad business. A company can't go giving out details about their clients. I would never do such a thing in my business. Tagget likes to dangle precariously from the precipice of legality, but his people are surprisingly loyal. I guarantee you no matter how many phone calls I make, I won't be able to get anyone at the company to tell me who was buying termites."

Yvette huffed. "I told you we needed to demand. I am a pirate. I will simply threaten or steal until I learn what I need."

Lina winced. Yvette's impulsive nature was not suited to a problem like this. Lina wanted to offer a better solution than committing crimes against a powerful man of questionable morals. But Yvette had popped another biscuit into her mouth, and the sugar was now on both lips and her fingers, and Lina's brain was turning to mush.

Her fingers tightened on her teacup. What the hell was wrong with her? She'd had plenty of past lovers. She'd even licked food off of some of them. Why was this particular woman so damned distracting? Why was it so hard to look away?

Yvette caught her staring. Holding Lina's gaze, she deliberately licked her fingers clean. One. By. One.

Lina nearly groaned.

"Miss Captain Redbeard?"

Lola's question broke the spell. Lina drew back, belatedly realizing she'd been leaning perilously close to Yvette.

"Are you and the other pirate lady in love?" Lola wondered. "I think she was making that kissy face, like Daddy does to Mommy."

Yvette turned crimson.

"We are friends," Lina blurted. "Just friends."

"Oui." Yvette had gone rigid and her voice was frosty. "Friends." She hopped up from her seat and carried her empty teacup to the tray. An uneaten biscuit remained on her saucer. She didn't pick it up. "We should go begin arrangements for the girls. Enemies could be following us."

"If any enemies make even the slightest attempt to harm anyone in or near my home, they will deeply regret it." Sabine's tone was so fierce, Lina believed her.

"Yvette is right." Lina rose from her seat. "We should go. We'll want to discuss our next steps with the crew."

"There is no discussion," Yvette snapped. "We are going to St. Louis to pick up Olga, then we will go to Tagget Industries and learn what we need."

She was angry again, and it was definitely Lola's curiosity that had caused the reaction.

Lina was a bit angry too—with herself. They'd been too obvious about their desires in public. They were violating the contract. And then she'd lied.

Which wasn't too horrible. Everyone lied at times. But this lie sat uncomfortably in her belly. Lina had friends. The pirate crew were rapidly becoming her friends, Sabine was a friend, and Nora would drop everything and run to help if Lina called. These were important, cherished relationships.

But Yvette didn't fit into that category. They were friendly, but not quite friends. Lovers, but only under strict conditions. Yvette meant something to Lina, though. Something that left her lustful and a bit perplexed.

Yvette made an imperious gesture and headed for the door. "We will return shortly with the girls," she called.

Lina hurried after, plagued by a burgeoning sensation that she had already misstepped. If she wasn't careful, someone would get hurt.

And she had no idea whether that someone would be Yvette or herself.

18

OLGA WALKED DOWN the front stairs of the doctor's elegant St. Louis townhouse and accepted a teary embrace from Angelique. Yvette left them to chatter away in a mix of French and German and went to shake Nora's hand.

"You do good work, Doctor. Olga is looking well."

"I'll tell you what I told her." Nora's sunny smile softened her stern doctor's voice. "No adventures for at least two weeks. She should continue with a spoonful of medicine twice a day until the bottle is empty. Lots of rest, good food, and no heavy lifting."

Yvette nodded. "I'll assign her appropriate tasks for a few weeks. And I will recommend your services for any of my contacts who need a biomechanologist."

Nora chuckled. "I continue to bolster my reputation as doctor to pirates."

"A worthy occupation."

"I'm glad you agree. Safe travels." Nora's smile faded slightly. "You're certain you won't stay for lunch? I have plenty of tea and coffee, and we can send for sandwiches for the whole crew."

Yvette's stomach rumbled at the mention of food. She hadn't really been eating right over the past several days.

Mostly snacks snatched in between shifts at the helm. Her life had been a non-stop cycle of fly, sleep, fly, sleep. It was good. The busier she was, the safer her heart was. She hadn't had much time to fantasize about Lina or berate herself for the way she'd flirted while at Sabine's house.

"We must go," she replied. "I don't want to bring enemies here, and I have business in New York." Yvette paused. "Does your luxene mogul husband have a connection with Tagget Industries?"

Nora's eyes widened. "Of course. Tagget owns Pure-Lux, Owen's biggest customer, and he's also done security for us."

Yvette bounced on the balls of her feet. "Excellent! Can Owen help me? I need to know who ordered a certain product from Tagget Industries recently. If he knows this Tagget person, he can ask."

Nora's brow wrinkled. "They're not really friends. And Owen wouldn't want to misuse a business connection. He can be very… lawful. I think he's still recovering from our misadventures earlier this year."

The same refusal they'd gotten from Sabine's duke. It seemed barging in and demanding was truly Yvette's best option. She'd make it work. Despite all the recent troubles, her crew was alive and together, and they'd managed their rescue of the girls. Somehow, she continued to succeed as captain, and she wasn't going to let that end now.

She inclined her head to Nora. "Thank you, Doctor. You will always be an honorary member of our crew."

With that, she spun and strode off for her ship.

"So you decided to stay with the pirates?" Nora's turquoise eyes were wide with undisguised curiosity. "You'll have to tell me all about it next time you visit."

"I've been useful to them," Lina replied. "And they've become friends. It's nice that I can be of assistance."

Nora grinned. "Your chance to be a hero?"

Lina flinched. "What? No!"

"It's not a bad thing. I save people for a living, you know. And Owen wouldn't hesitate to put on armor and charge into battle if he thought it would protect a loved one." Nora chuckled. "Which is maybe a bit excessive, but he means well."

Lina straightened her shoulders and adopted a professional tone. "There's a difference between wanting to do good and imagining oneself as a fairy-tale hero." She'd given up on that nonsense years ago, after the debacle with Emily. No one—not even Nora—needed to know about that foolishness. "Like you, I try to live a life where I can help people with my skills and knowledge. Yvette can fly around in her airship and her fancy red coat attempting to rescue damsels in distress. But that's not the life for me. Soon enough, I'll return to my quiet existence in Savannah."

Lina called up an image of her house in her mind, but the memories it conjured were only negative. Nosy neighbors asking once again why she hadn't "found a nice young man." Fellow scholars dismissing her papers or talking down to her. Lovers flitting in and out of her life because an affair with a Feminist Lesbian Psychologist excited them, but was too scandalous to risk more than a few covert meetings.

"I might need to make a few changes, of course," she amended hastily. "But that's why travel with the pirates is a good thing. I'm opening my mind to new experiences and helping people in need. I'm sure when I return home life will be even better than before."

Nora folded her arms across her chest. "Are you trying to convince me or yourself?"

Lina's jaw clenched as she fought to keep a neutral expression. "Merely stating the facts." She glanced over her shoulder. "I should go. The crew will have need of me."

"Of course. Safe travels, Lina." Nora offered a hug, and Lina accepted.

"Thank you. I'll visit longer next time."

Nora gave her a final squeeze, then let go. "I'll hold you to that. Farewell. And Lina?"

Lina paused in the act of turning away. "Yes?"

"Don't be afraid to go after everything you want. Don't settle for less. You deserve it all. I'm here in St. Louis, running a wholly not-for-profit clinic, because the man I love was willing to invest not only his money, but his time and effort, into ensuring I could pursue the career I find most fulfilling. If you find people like that while you're flying around the world, hang on to them. And I will always have tea and an extra room here. And biscuits, if you bring the pirates with you."

The memory of Yvette's sugar-coated lips blazed in Lina's mind. "We'll see. Thank you, Nora. You're a true friend. I love you."

The affectionate words felt odd on Lina's tongue. She couldn't even remember the last time she'd said anything of the sort, to anyone. Today, though, they were necessary. And right.

Nora beamed. "I love you too. Now go, before the pirates leave you behind."

"The crew leaves no woman behind," Lina replied. It was only later, as she grasped the rope ladder to climb aboard the ship, that she realized she hadn't merely blurted out the words by rote. She believed them.

Interesting.

19

*Y*VETTE ROSE AT DAWN the next morning to take over at the helm for the approach to New York City. The last few hours of any journey were always her favorite, full of the excitement of arrival and the challenge of landing. Today was particularly pleasant. The sun blazed bright and the blustery autumn air gave her plenty to concentrate on as she maneuvered through the busy skies in search of an appropriate tether location. She was tempted to drop a line and tie La Liberté to the statue of the same name, but that would clash with her purpose for flying straight into Manhattan. They needed information now, before another attack came. Yvette wasn't going to waste time landing at the airfield and taking a train into the city proper.

Besides, part of the fun of being a pirate was ignoring laws that inconvenienced you. Illegally mooring an airship to a private building was a rite of passage. Since this was her first time in New York, she didn't intend to miss her opportunity.

Chantal jogged over, spyglass in hand. "Found it! You were right about the Lower Manhattan location. Financial district. It's not a fancy building. Red brick with minimal stone trim, eight stories tall. There's already an airship tethered to it, so we will need to choose another building nearby."

Yvette let a mischievous grin slide over her face. "Does

"

the stock exchange have an airship tether?" If she was going to thumb her nose at the law, she might as well do it in style.

Chantal giggled. "I'll go look."

The girl darted off, but Yvette didn't remain undisturbed for long. Lina came striding up to the bridge, her long skirt swirling in the wind. She wore a black suit jacket today, hiding her suspenders. Which was a good thing, because every time she wore them—most days—Yvette wanted to either touch them where they curved around Lina's breasts or tug them off and leave them dangling in a suggestion of dishabille.

"You aren't going to set down in the middle of Central Park, are you?" Lina asked, speaking as if Yvette were one of her clients to be psychoanalyzed.

"Non. It is a fine idea, and would be good for the reputation of Captain Redbeard, but our quarry is downtown."

"Quarry?" Lina's eyebrows rose. "Yvette, as a friend, I must once again ask you to reconsider."

That was more or less the only thing Lina had said to Yvette since they'd left England. Probably because Lina insisted on bringing up the subject, while Yvette refused to discuss it. She'd completely exhausted her supply of "urgent captain's matters" for abruptly ending conversations.

Today, the words "as a friend" added a new dimension of annoyance to this particular encounter. Were they friends at all? Lina hadn't acted even slightly perturbed that Yvette was making herself either busy or scarce. Every greeting came with a polite smile and a breezy tone. As if they were casual acquaintances. As if Lina had entirely forgotten the passionate interlude in Yvette's cabin.

Yvette refused to meet Lina's gaze because that was the easiest way to play level-headed captain. It was silly to still be hurt by what Lina had said days ago in Sabine's house. It was silly to be hurt by it at all. Lina had said the sensible thing. Of course she had.

But why had she blurted it out as if to hide something? As

if she were ashamed? They'd been among friends, with no need to worry that someone might unfairly judge them for a socially taboo relationship.

The same old questions caromed around in Yvette's brain. *Was it your fault? Were you not good enough? Or too much? Always too much. Too curious. Too impulsive. Too emotional.*

"Look," Lina sighed, halting Yvette's moping, but not improving her mood. "There is a sensible way to go about this. We can gather information on the company and the owner. Evan Tagget is famous. Or perhaps infamous, given that spying incident. There are articles about him all over old newspapers and magazines. All we need is a library. Then I can analyze him and determine the best course of action for persuading him to give us the information we need."

"A knife to the throat is persuasive."

"That's not funny."

Yvette gripped the wheel and stared straight ahead. "It wasn't a joke."

"Please."

The word was so gentle, Yvette almost flinched. Then Lina laid a hand on Yvette's shoulder and she did flinch.

"Please reconsider," Lina murmured. "I don't want to see you get hurt."

Yvette's heart jolted. Maybe she'd misread Lina's behavior. Perhaps her calm politeness was her way of trying to be friends. Or was the touch an indication that she still wished to be lovers?

Why do you care? You shouldn't care so much.

Friends or lovers. Either one was a danger to her heart. If she let herself slide back into the girl she had once been, it would put her crew at risk. It would threaten everything she'd built.

"I don't want anyone to get hurt," she retorted. "That is why I need the information. I can handle one stuffy businessman."

Lina stepped away and rubbed her temple. "Fine. But I'm going with you."

"That is acceptable."

A mere half-hour later, Yvette and Lina walked together into the atrium of Tagget Industries headquarters.

"May I help you?" inquired the person seated behind the front desk. They sported a cheerful smile, a shock of henna-red hair, an androgynously-cut suit coat of pale blue silk, and a fluffy white cravat.

Yvette took an immediate liking to the place. Perhaps Tagget would be reasonable, since he appeared to allow his employees to dress however they wanted.

"We are here to see Mr. Tagget," she announced.

The receptionist frowned. "He has no appointments today."

"We will only be a few minutes. Can you direct us to his office?"

"No." The word was punctuated with a straightening spine. Did the receptionist double as a bodyguard? They weren't terribly large. Yvette gave herself even odds in a fight.

Lina stepped in before Yvette could formulate a properly intimidating reply. "Could you ask Mr. Tagget if he will see us? My name is Catalina Navarro, psychological therapist, and I am a friend of Dr. Eleanor Taylor-Cassidy and Her Grace, the Duchess of Hartleigh."

"I can take your name and number, but—"

A crackling sound cut off the receptionist's brusque words. "You may send them up, Price," a man's voice said through a speaker. "Thank you for your vigilance. Please have Captain Redbeard leave her weapons in the safe box."

"Yes, sir." Price pushed a button, and a heavy drawer popped out of one side of the reception desk. "You may deposit your weapons here, Captain. Then take the far elevator. It will open for you."

Yvette looked at Lina, who shook her head.

"I don't like this," Lina said. "How does he know who you are? I only gave my name."

Price chuckled. "Oh, Mr. Tagget knows everyone important."

Important? Yvette's chest puffed up with pure pleasure. She was important! She pulled out her pistols and her knife and placed them all in the drawer.

"Ooh," Price crooned. "Antique flintlocks in stunning condition! I'll make certain to keep them safe."

That answered the bodyguard question. Yvette beamed at the receptionist and headed for the small, unlabeled elevator in the corner of the atrium.

The doors opened at her approach to reveal a sleek steel interior with just enough room for two people to stand.

"Very smart," she applauded. "Even if enemies get to the lift, they can only go up by twos. Limits the possibility of attack."

"A fortress," Lina groaned, though she followed Yvette into the elevator. "I'm not getting a favorable impression of this man."

"He probably heard that," Yvette pointed out.

Lina sagged against the wall.

The lift doors slid closed, and they shot upward at a speed so rapid Yvette's stomach felt like it dropped to the floor. In moments, the elevator reached its destination and the doors opened to reveal an unadorned, windowless hallway. Three closed doors punctuated the otherwise empty wall. The center door bore a small silver plaque that said only, "Evan Tagget."

Yvette strode over and seized the handle, pleased to find that it turned in her hand. She pushed the door open and walked in without bothering to knock.

A pale, dark-haired man in a black suit sat behind a desk, stacking slim wooden blocks one atop the other to make some sort of bizarre spiral pattern. "What can I do for you, Captain?" he asked, without looking away from his… project.

"I need to know who ordered the termites." She spoke as if to her crew, commanding but not angry or cruel.

Tagget did look up now. "The what?"

"The termites. The tiny metal bugs with the drill heads."

"Ah." He added another block to his creation. "The micro-drillers. An excellent design. I gave that engineer a large bonus."

"Who bought them?" Yvette demanded. "And not La Capitaine. Who else?"

Tagget caught her gaze and held it. "I'm afraid I can't tell you that."

Yvette shifted her weight and fought the urge to pound a fist on the desk. "I need to know."

Tagget shrugged. "I don't give out private client information. No one wants to do business with a snitch."

Yvette sniffed and turned to Lina. "Didn't you say he spied on people? What's the difference?"

"It's a power thing," Lina explained. "He won't give information to us for the same reason he steals it from others. He likes the control. I suspect it's some deep-seated sense of insecurity."

"Yes, yes, just like my excessive number of pillows." Tagget placed the last of the blocks atop his structure. "I am aware of my personal neuroses, I have no wish to discuss my tragic past, and I haven't seen my wife in two days. Therefore, as charming as you ladies are, I will have to ask you to leave. The office is closed."

"It's barely past eleven." Lina's brow crinkled in confusion. "I would have assumed you work long hours."

"I am highly eccentric." Tagget yanked out one of the bottom-most blocks, and the entire creation collapsed down into a surprisingly tidy pile. "Ha! Look at that." He grinned like a schoolboy and spoke into a device that looked like the mouthpiece end of a telephone. "Price, phone Dawson and tell him I love his idea and to build a 1/12 scale prototype from the metal scraps. I will be leaving shortly. Do you know if Violet is back on Dauntless yet?"

"She is not, sir," Price's crackly voice replied.

"Damned long-winded art critics. Put in my usual lunch order to Delmonico's and have it delivered to the ship. Plus extra chocolate cake and hot tea for Violet. She'll be tired and hungry when she arrives. Thank you."

"Mr. Tagget—" Yvette tried again, but he cut her off.

"Apologies, my brash and plucky pirate. Tagget Industries employs thousands, and the funds it generates are feeding orphans and supporting progressive reforms. I will not put my people at risk. I'm certain you can find your information elsewhere." He rose from his seat. "Good day."

Yvette couldn't even think of a reply. This was the time where the obvious course of action would be to vault over the desk, pin him to the wall, and threaten to beat him senseless unless he told her what she wanted.

Except she liked him. He was both very much and not at all what she'd expected, and that intrigued her. In other circumstances, she would try to befriend him.

Yvette took a step forward, but before she could even pretend to threaten Tagget, he spun around, put a hand to the wall, and pushed open a secret door. In a flash, he was gone, the door swinging firmly shut behind him.

"Merde!" Yvette raced to the wall and pushed, but the secret door was locked tight. She couldn't even see it, it fit so neatly into the paneling. Gritting her teeth, she turned back to Lina. "Now what?"

"I have no idea," Lina replied. "I told you this wouldn't work. And now I don't think we can even try a persuasive argument by telephone or letter. He'll simply ignore anything coming from us."

Yvette spun away, fighting the rush of tears welling in her

eyes. So much for continuing to succeed. And she wasn't just a failure. She was a disappointment. To Lina. To everyone.

She marched out the door to find the elevator open and waiting. Lina's footsteps sounded behind her.

"Do you have any ideas?" Lina asked.

Yvette almost snorted. That had to be Lina trying to be nice. She couldn't possibly want to go along with another of Yvette's plans after this pointless endeavor.

"Tagget seems to love his wife," she grumbled. "Maybe we could kidnap her."

Lina didn't reply until the elevator doors closed behind them. "Honestly, that might work. Not that I would advise it."

Yvette turned slowly to face her. "I wouldn't do it anyway. I liked him."

Lina had been stern-faced for the entirety of this misadventure, but now she smiled. "Of course you did. You both possess deep loyalties, but enjoy swimming in morally gray waters."

Yvette had to look away again. That pretty much summed her up, she supposed. Too bad to be good. Too good to be bad. She didn't fit anywhere.

She never had.

20

*L*INA DASHED ACROSS the street after Yvette, narrowly avoiding an onrushing steam car. The driver honked, and Yvette made a rude gesture in reply. They'd been in Manhattan for less than an hour, and already she strode around as if she owned the place.

"Maybe you could attempt to befriend Tagget," Lina suggested. "If he believed he could trust you, perhaps he would share the information."

Yvette cast a frown at Lina, but didn't slow her rapid pace. "How could I do that?"

"I don't know yet. It was only an idea, since you said you liked him. You could befriend his wife, too. She's an artist, and according to rumor she's terribly scandalous. I expect you might like her."

Yvette shrugged. "I am not good at making friends."

"Nonsense." Yvette had plenty of friends. All the women on her ship. Sabine. Nora. Her contacts in various ports. "You befriended me easily enough."

Yvette's brows knit together, but she didn't reply.

"We are friends, aren't we?" Lina prompted. She'd been trying for days now to behave cordially without flirting. Friends in public, lovers in private. It seemed the best way to adhere to the contract they'd signed.

"Perhaps," Yvette finally answered.

So much for easing Lina's doubts. Maybe Yvette couldn't quite categorize their relationship either. It could explain her recent avoidance.

Or maybe she's simply done with you, as both friend and lover.

No. That couldn't be. They'd been getting on well this morning, even when they disagreed. Working together.

"I cannot spend time making friends with rich people," Yvette declared. "Our enemy could catch up at any moment."

Lina nodded. She needed to stop trying to analyze everything and just accept this peculiar partnership as it was. "Abandon the termite question and make a new plan?"

"Yes. Set a trap."

"Sounds dangerous. I hate it." Before Yvette could argue, Lina added, "But it's better than letting them attack us unprepared."

Yvette grinned. "I like that you are saying 'us.' You are really part of the crew now."

"I..." *No woman left behind.* "I suppose—"

A large, dark shadow passed overhead. Lina looked up instinctively, expecting a low-flying airship or an ominous raincloud.

"Hell and damn and blast!" Yvette cursed, breaking into a run.

Lina stumbled after, glancing up as she ran, trying to form a clear picture of the… thing circling above them. It was made of metal, with wings and multiple limbs, but with the sun reflecting off its surface, she couldn't make out more than that.

"Look out!" someone shouted.

"A monster!"

"Run! Run!"

The creature swooped lower, then dove for the street, coming in so fast Lina covered her head and ducked. The ground trembled as it landed somewhere behind her.

Lina and Yvette both staggered to a halt and whirled

around. The dragon was larger than any Lina had seen, at least twenty feet tall, with huge canvas wings stretched between iron bars. As it rose up onto its hind legs, the wings folded closed. Its body had an ursine shape, its front paws tipped with enormous, curving claws.

"Is that the bear that attacked you in Paris?" Lina gasped.

The monster swiped a paw at a nearby building, scoring the brick and shattering windows. Pedestrians screamed and ran, some racing for doorways, others waving hands and shouting for cabs.

"Bigger!" Yvette shouted. "And the Paris bear had no wings. A prototype." She seized Lina's arm. "Hurry, we must get to the ship."

The bear-dragon stomped down the street—away from Lina and Yvette, thank God—knocking down streetlamps and damaging more buildings. A terrified driver leapt from his steam car as the bear lumbered toward him. The creature lifted the abandoned vehicle and flung it halfway down the block, giving a roar of fury.

Lina ran.

The crew on the ship had the cargo lift lowered and the ship ready for takeoff by the time Lina and Yvette arrived.

"We saw the monster," Kaina greeted them the moment the lift reached the deck. "Is it after us?"

Yvette shook her head. "I think it is here to destroy. To cause chaos. We must stop it. Ready the cannon."

"Cannon?" Lina stumbled from the lift. "We have a cannon?"

Yvette sniffed. "Of course we have a cannon. We are pirates." She waved one hand. "It is an ugly, uncivilized thing, but we will use it if we must."

"You can't fire a cannon in New York City!"

"There may be other ways to destroy the monster, but we must be prepared. Find a safe location. I am taking the helm."

Lina followed her. "Give me a task. I'd rather help."

"Then take the spyglass. Watch the monster while we follow it. Look for weak points."

Lina raced to the bow, lifted the spyglass from its mount, and trained it on the city streets as La Liberté lifted off. The bear-dragon wasn't hard to find. It barreled up Broadway, leaving a trail of destruction in its wake. She could find no obvious weaknesses, but she did take a good long look at its claws. The steel talons bore scratches from use, but no sign of any foreign substances coating the tips. No fear of the poison that had hurt Olga, then. Still, a single swipe from those paws could easily be fatal.

The creature was fast, too. Already it was nearing the beautiful new skyscraper everyone had dubbed the Flatiron Building for its triangular shape. Most likely it would continue up 5th Avenue toward Central Park. With luck, it would focus its wrath on the homes of the rich and famous. They could afford it.

Lina rushed back to the bridge to update Yvette. The captain had steered the ship parallel to 5th Avenue and now had her on a slow but steady descent.

"The cannon is down in the hold, at the bow," Yvette explained. "If we can get low enough, the crew can shoot the beast from behind."

Lina trained the spyglass on the bear again. Any pedestrians in its path were already running for cover. "You're certain the weapon is accurate enough?"

"From this distance, oui."

"Okay." Lina took a calming breath. "If you can get low enough between the buildings, then shoot before it kills anyone."

"That was my plan." Yvette tapped a button on the control panel. "Aim the cannon. Fire on my signal," her amplified voice echoed across the ship. She moved the wheel in tiny increments, staring straight ahead, her brow furrowed in concentration. "Ten seconds to firing position."

Lina's shoulders tensed. She clutched the spyglass and tried to hold it steady as she watched their mechanical quarry.

"Five. Four."

The bear-dragon turned.

"Wait!"

Yvette stopped counting. "Hold positions," she commanded, pulling at the controls to place the ship in hover.

Down on the ground, the bear dug its claws into the brick of a building and began to climb. Lina let the spyglass drop.

"We can't shoot. Not while it's climbing." Her gaze drifted up the building. Sixteen stories tall, Renaissance Revival architecture, connected to its former rival next door. Damnation. "That's the Waldorf-Astoria."

"The hotel?"

"Yes." *The* hotel, in fact. Famous. Fashionable. Massively popular. "It will be crammed with people. We can't fire at it."

The bear continued its ascent, gouging the walls and breaking windows. If it got inside, there would be carnage.

Lina nearly threw the spyglass. "Goddammit! We have to stop it. We can't let it break into the hotel. But if we shoot it, we could kill people."

Yvette muttered something in French. "Zahra, to the helm," she called. "Kaina, I need a wing pack and a six-shooter."

Lina rounded on her. Not again. No way was she letting Yvette hatch another impulsive plan without explanation.

"What is a wing pack? What are you doing?"

Yvette kept her focus on the controls. La Liberté began to rise, keeping pace with the dragon climbing the hotel.

"I am going to kill the monster." Yvette finally looked at Lina, her eyes hard as ice. "Don't try to stop me."

21

APPARENTLY, she had to do this herself.

Yvette gave the helm to Zahra and rushed down to take the wing pack from Kaina. The crew had jumped to obey her commands. They wanted to help. Unfortunately, the universe seemed determined to make Yvette handle things alone.

"You're sure about this, Captain?" Kaina asked. "We have three more wing packs below."

Yvette slung the pack onto her back and fastened the harness around her waist and chest. "A surprise attack will work better with only one woman. Don't follow unless I fail."

The click of Lina's hard-soled shoes announced her presence before she even spoke. "Yvette, you can't do this!"

Yvette popped her wings open. Like the bear-dragon's, they were made of stretched canvas and modeled on the wings of a bat. She made a cute bat, to be perfectly honest.

Lina ducked under the wings and planted herself in front of Yvette. "You'll get yourself killed."

Lina's scowl should have been fearsome, but Yvette found herself smiling beneath it. What a lovely sight it was, seeing prim, level-headed Lina unraveled. She was a woman of deep passions, and every time they rose to the surface Yvette's body responded with a jolt of excitement. Even furious Lina enticed her, with those flashing dark eyes and flushed cheeks. Yvette's skin heated at the memory of their time in bed together.

A good memory to hold on to, in the event she failed to vanquish the monster.

"I *will* destroy it," she declared. "Kaina, the gun?"

Lina seized Yvette's wrist. "Can those wings even hold you? Don't do this!"

"I've used the wings many times. Step aside before I run out of time."

Kaina reached past Lina to hand Yvette the revolver. The heavy American gun didn't suit her small hands, but it was powerful enough to pierce the beast's metal hide.

"Its main reservoir is almost certainly in the torso," Kaina said. "Rubber tubes will run out into its limbs. The hydraulics will fail without proper pressure. Make as many holes as you can."

"I will. Pick me up when I have killed it." Yvette stepped around Lina and climbed up on the rail, trying to block out the sounds of Lina's protests.

"Yvette, please. It's too dange—"

"I am not a reckless fool," Yvette snarled, and launched herself off the ship.

The glide down to the hotel took only moments. She set down gently atop the mansard roof of the tallest tower, neatly avoiding the spikes of the decorative ironwork. Landing on a stationary target was child's play.

See, Miss Navarro? Look how competent I am.

Yvette gave herself a little shake. If she wanted to remain competent, she needed to stay on task. This was her chance to play the hero.

Kill the monster. Save the city. Get the girl.

Yvette raised her gun and tread carefully across the roof. Below her, a vast rooftop garden spread across most of the building, neatly shielded from the noise and bustle of the city below. Amid the potted ferns and neoclassical decor, guests promenaded, mingled, and enjoyed an outdoor lunch on this pretty autumn day. A few people pointed up at the strange woman with wings and the airship above her.

"Putain de bordel de merde!"

Fuck, fuck, fuck. There had to be a hundred or more people in the garden, blissfully oblivious to the creature climbing toward them. If the bear reached the garden, there would be a bloodbath.

"Run!" she shouted, though she wasn't sure how far her voice would carry. "Inside! Go!"

A massive claw curled around the bulbous dome of the nearest corner turret. No more time. Yvette spread her feet and grasped the revolver with both hands, praying she would have a clear shot from her higher position.

A second claw stabbed into the dome, tearing off a sheet of the copper roof and hurling it to the streets below. The bear threw back its head and roared in triumph.

A woman screamed, but no one ran. The whole crowd stood like statues, frozen in either shock or terror.

"Climb higher, you bastard," Yvette growled. The decorative dome blocked too much of the bear, and she needed a shot at the torso. Her bullets were limited. None could be wasted. If she let these people die, it would be the biggest failure of her life. And Lina would see it all.

God, what a ridiculous worry. She couldn't shake it off, though. Somehow everything would be worse if Lina knew all the gory details. Maybe because she was so proper and perfect and *right* all the time. Lina probably would have landed in the ideal spot to shoot the bear.

The bear roared again, flinging debris down into the garden. More screams went up. The people at last seemed to grasp the danger, and most began to scramble from their seats. A few continued to gape in rapt fascination, drinks in hand. One man raised a camera.

And Yvette still couldn't find a decent shot.

Keeping a tight grip on her pistol, she stepped up onto the decorative rail. If she swooped down into the garden, she could fire at the monster from a better angle, plus keep it away from people if it leapt down.

Yvette jumped, her gaze fixed on a patch of rooftop clear of people. Halfway down, she jerked to an ungainly halt, her head snapping painfully back. She dangled in midair, her right wing caught on something.

Caught *by* something.

The monster tossed her like a doll, catching her in its opposite paw and crushing her wings beyond repair. Below her lay nothing but pavement and more than seventy meters of empty air.

Her scream was lost beneath the bear's bellow.

No. Oh, no, please, no.

This couldn't be happening. Lina would kill her. If, somehow, she managed not to be eaten or thrown to the ground, Lina would absolutely kill her for this ill-considered, futile plan.

Yvette forced herself to look up into the face of the beast. She still had her gun. If she killed it, she'd tumble to her death. But she would still save all the people.

The bear shook her, and she clutched the gun until the metal dug into her flesh.

You are not Yvette. You are the dread pirate Redbeard. You are afraid of nothing.

She took aim at the monster's right eye. If it had controls in its head, like a brain, perhaps she could disable it without damaging the hydraulics. As long as it kept its grip on the building and on her, she still had a chance.

She fired. The bear howled and thrashed, nearly slamming her into the spire topping the battered onion dome.

The spire.

Yvette's stomach churned, and her neck and shoulders ached from the shaking, but suddenly the discomfort was welcome. It meant she was alive. And, just maybe, she could stay that way.

She took aim again, firing at the left eye. Blinded, the monster screamed in confusion and fury.

Yvette focused on her own body as the bear waved her about, trying to keep her senses through the nausea. She unclipped her wing harness where it crossed her chest and wriggled her right arm free of the apparatus. Keeping the six-shooter tight in her left hand, she grasped the dangling harness strap with her right and looked for her opportunity.

The bear tore another chuck from the roof and flung it into the air. Bile rose in Yvette's throat when she heard the distant crash of copper against pavement.

That won't be me. It won't be me.

She squirmed and tried to reach out as she came within a hand's span of the roof.

Closer. Closer. Please.

With an earsplitting scream, the monster slammed the paw holding Yvette down onto the roof. The impact jarred every bone in her body, but the whole of her being was honed in on her prize. As the bear lifted her again, she lunged for the spire, hooking her harness onto a decorative wrought-iron protrusion.

The unexpected restraint confused the monster, and its grip on Yvette relaxed. Seizing her chance, she fired twice into the center of the creature's chest. A quick adjustment to her aim, and she fired her penultimate shot directly through the elbow joint of the arm holding her.

The bear quivered, then went still. Clear fluid oozed from the bullet holes. The claws wrapped around Yvette began to uncurl.

She took a final shot at the monster's torso, then flung the revolver aside and pried herself free from the beast's steel fingers.

The bear teetered. Yvette held her breath.

The monster let out one final, plaintive groan, then toppled from the building.

Yvette's entire body went limp. Half-clipped into her harness, she dangled from the spire, swaying slowly in the breeze. Alive.

"Captain!"

Three pirates with wing packs glided into the rooftop garden.

"Don't move! We're coming for you!"

Yvette closed her eyes and concentrated on her breathing, trying to slow her racing pulse. She'd done it. She'd succeeded. It hadn't been pretty, but she'd accomplished the task she'd set herself, and there'd been no casualties, pirate or civilian.

By the time her crew helped her down to the safety of the garden, she'd recovered enough that her knees didn't buckle and her hands only shook a tiny bit. A leisurely ride on the cargo lift settled her nerves even further. She stepped onto the deck with her customary swagger, prepared to meet Lina's furious glower with confidence.

"The bear-dragon is dead," she announced.

The crew cheered.

Except Lina, naturally. The therapist looked unusually pale, and she held her fists clenched at her sides. She stalked toward Yvette, then made a brusque gesture at the stairs leading below.

"Downstairs. Now."

Yvette sniffed. "Very well."

It made more sense to argue in private, she supposed. Better for morale not to question the captain in front of everyone. If Lina was considering such things, she couldn't be too troubled. Yvette would simply let her rant, then politely point out that the plan had worked and sometimes split-second decisions were necessary. Then they could return to being... whatever it was they were.

Yvette led the way to her cabin, turned on the lights, and

shut the door for maximum privacy. Keeping her chin up, she looked Lina in the eye.

"We are alone. You may proceed."

Lina backed Yvette into the wall and kissed her.

22

Warm. Solid. Alive.

Lina pinned Yvette against the wall, trapping her between both arms, desperate to hold her here, to keep her from slipping away ever again.

She was here. Alive. Real. And she tasted like heaven.

For an instant, Yvette was stiff beneath the kiss, and Lina nearly pulled away, afraid she'd misread some signal. But then the pirate wound her arms around Lina's neck and relaxed into the embrace, her lips parting on a soft sigh.

Hot, desperate need coiled in Lina's belly. God, had any woman ever had such a perfect mouth? Yvette's lips were exactly the right size to fit against Lina's. Exactly the right shape to trace with a tongue. Exactly the right plumpness for a gentle little nibble.

Lina kissed with wild abandon, smothering every tiny noise Yvette made, grinding their bodies together. Yvette responded in kind, her lips and tongue exploring with the same chaotic energy she exhibited in every aspect of her life. She squirmed, dug her fingers into Lina's hair, and kissed harder.

It wasn't enough. Lina wanted more. *Needed* more. In fact, she wasn't certain she could ever get enough, even if she kissed Yvette like this every day for the rest of her life. Which was ridiculous. Surely this seemingly unending craving was merely a reaction to a high level of stress.

Think later; fuck now.

It felt like the most sensible thought Lina had ever had. She stepped away from the wall, pulling Yvette with her. They needed the bed. Needed these clothes off immediately. If Lina couldn't get her hands on Yvette's body, skin-to-skin, she might actually go out of her mind. She ached to touch every part of her, taste every part of her. To feel the heat of her breath and the pounding rhythm of her heart.

Yvette staggered out of Lina's arms. Her eyes were glazed with molten desire, her hair mussed, and cheeks flushed. She fumbled with the buttons of her vest, then tossed it aside and yanked her shirt up over her head.

Lina scrambled for her own fastenings. She flung garments here and there, not even seeing where they fell. All that mattered was having Yvette's lithe body beneath her as soon as possible.

"I thought you were angry at me," Yvette gasped, as Lina tackled her onto the bed.

Lina lowered her head to nuzzle Yvette's breasts. She cupped the soft globes in her hands and flicked her tongue over one straining nipple. "I'm furious."

She slid her mouth down over the tight peak and tugged at it with increasingly vigorous sucks until Yvette let out a moan of delight.

"I should make you furious…" Yvette gasped out as Lina moved to the opposite breast, "…more often."

If Lina's mouth hadn't been more pleasurably engaged, she would have laughed. A heady surge of satisfaction filled her chest. She could amuse and titillate at the same time. And she was only getting started.

Lina eased herself down Yvette's body, pressing whisper-light kisses over her belly and settling comfortably between her thighs.

"You make me furious every damn day." Lina skimmed her fingers along the insides of Yvette's legs, teasing her way up to that pretty, pink quim, warm and slick with arousal. "Every. Damn. Day."

God, the heady scent of a woman's pleasure. Lina's whole body had begun to ache from the force of it. Yvette was infuriatingly intoxicating, in and out of bed. Annoying, stubborn, impulsive. Brave, daring, loyal.

Lina finally set her tongue to the soft folds of Yvette's labia, tasting the reality of her. It didn't entirely banish the memory of mechanical claws snatching her from the air, but it did spark another rush of relief. Yvette was in Lina's clutches now. And this time when she screamed, it was going to be for the right reasons.

Lina circled Yvette's clit with her tongue, then sucked on the taut bud. Slow and torturous would have to wait for another day. Right now, she needed to feel Yvette come and hear her sweet cries.

Yvette's hips bucked, and soon she was panting and digging her fingers into the bedding. Lina sucked harder, reveling in each squirm and moan.

Yes. That's my girl. My wild monster slayer. Show me what happens when all that energy inside you explodes.

She worked Yvette higher still, sliding a finger inside her and curling it to find the spot that made her gasp.

"L-Lina…" Her head lolled to one side, and she convulsed, letting out a cry that slowed to a whimper as Lina gentled her sucks.

When Yvette finally went boneless, Lina withdrew. She wiped her face on the bedsheets, then crawled up the bed until they lay side-by-side.

Yvette's blond waves splayed out every which way. Her skin glowed pink, and a few stray drops of perspiration glistened on her brow.

Lina kissed her. "Don't you ever do something so dangerous ever again," she scolded.

Yvette's sleepy gaze sharpened. "I should do such dangerous things every day, if this is my reward." A triumphant and decidedly smug smile spread clear across her face. "The fierce pirate saves the city and beds the most beautiful wench on the ship."

The muscles in Lina's cheeks twitched, trying to form a smile.

Don't.

She fought to keep her face impassive. A smile would imply that she might condone future reckless behavior. She couldn't do that. But at the same time, she couldn't summon up her anger under the force of Yvette's grin.

The pirate captain was justly proud of single-handedly destroying the monster. She'd made an impressive sight, wings on her back and a pistol in hand. Never giving up. Always thinking and improvising. Frustrating, yes. But also marvelous.

Yvette turned on her side and leaned in until Lina could feel her breath. "May I pleasure you, beautiful wench?"

Lina lost the battle against the smile. A naked, satisfied Yvette calling her beautiful was too irresistible. "Do your worst."

"Hmph." Yvette turned up her nose. "Another silly English saying. I will do my *best*." She climbed atop Lina and kissed her with as much hunger as when they'd been up against the wall, letting her hands meander over Lina's body.

Eventually, Yvette broke the kiss and lowered her head to stroke her tongue over one of Lina's nipples. "I think…" She blew a stream of cool air across the moistened flesh, making Lina's entire body clench. "I will do all the same things you did to me."

"Yes, please."

If Lina had known what Yvette intended, she might have added a caveat. The saucy pirate began to mimic everything

Lina had done, but with agonizing leisure. She lavished attention first on the right breast, then the left, ramping up the intensity of each lick and suck in such incremental bits that Lina wanted to scream in frustrated ecstasy.

"More. Please."

Yvette let Lina's nipple slide from between her lips and flashed a devilish smile. "Oui, ma belle. I have more for you. But you must be patient. Unless you do not want my best?"

"Just put your mouth on me, dammit. I need to feel you."

Yvette's cheeks flushed and her smile turned almost bashful. "I am happy that I please you."

And back she went, kissing along Lina's body with undisguised enthusiasm, creeping lower to nip and suck at the sensitive skin of her upper thighs.

Lina grasped the slats of the headboard to fend off the temptation to touch herself. As much as she longed to ease the throbbing ache between her legs, she couldn't bring herself to disrupt Yvette's ministrations.

It had to be Yvette. The woman was some incomprehensible mix of angel and devil, casting her victims into the fiery depths while smiling and playing sweet melodies on her harp. And Lina had fallen completely under her spell. She relished the burn, danced to Yvette's tune, and longed to bask in this glow forever, whether it was a heavenly aura or hellish flames.

Yvette's teeth scraped over Lina's skin, and she moaned.

Yes. Mark me. Make me remember your touch every time I feel that place tomorrow.

Words wouldn't come, so Lina arched her back, begging silently. At long last, Yvette pressed her mouth to Lina's sex, sweeping over her with languid strokes, dipping inside her to stoke the fire hotter.

Lina's mind became a blur of need. When Yvette's lips closed around her clit, she rocked upward into the sensation, her fingers clenching, her toes curling. Yes, yes, yes. More,

more, more. Her whole body moved in rhythm with every pulse of unbearably perfect suction.

Harder. Faster. Harder. Faster.

Helpless, desperate noises fell from her lips. Her eyes squeezed closed. Every muscle from head to toe tensed in anticipation.

And then she was soaring, twisting and turning as the pleasure exploded through her.

"Fuck. Me," she gasped. She flung her arms wide and lay staring up at the ceiling, chest heaving.

Yvette sat up. "I believe I already did."

Lina managed a short laugh. "Yes. Quite well." She pressed the back of her hand to her brow. "I can barely move. We should do it again sometime."

"Many times." Yvette smiled, then looked suddenly away. She stretched out on the bed beside Lina but not facing her. "Let us rest, but then we must work. Our enemy will be angry."

Lina turned her face into the pillow. Devil take their blasted enemies! But Yvette was right. One way or another, they needed to solve this problem. Maybe then Yvette would stop putting herself in perilous situations and Lina could relax for more than a few minutes. Already, her post-coital euphoria was waning. For some reason—her brain remained too distracted to determine why—this made her want to punch something. She closed her eyes and tried to focus on her body and the warmth of Yvette lying beside her.

A frantic knocking at the door ruined any chance at recovering a sense of peace and satisfaction.

"Captain?" a voice called. "I'm sorry to disturb you, but another ship is signaling to us. They claim to have a message for you from a Mr. Tagget. Shall we try to scare them off, or let them approach?"

Yvette rolled out of bed. "We will have to rest later," she said to Lina. "It seems you are not the only one to admire my victory."

Lina sniffed. "His admiration had better involve keeping his damned clothes on."

"It had better involve the termite buyer." Yvette tossed her hair, then bent to pick up her clothes. "Or else I may use the cannon after all."

23

JAGGET KISSED YVETTE'S KNUCKLES. "Au revoir, my charming corsair."

She beamed at him, then kissed him on both cheeks. Some Americans knew how to be properly debonair. From now on, she would consider Evan an honorary Parisian.

Yvette turned to Violet and kissed her goodbye as well. "I will visit your art exhibition in Paris next summer. And perhaps I will see you before that, when I deliver a shipment."

Violet rolled her eyes, but Evan chuckled. Yvette didn't doubt they would both enjoy the tax-free Cognac.

Yvette picked up her parcel before giving a final nod of farewell and setting off for her ship. Perhaps her day hadn't begun as she'd intended, but this afternoon had been nothing short of magical. First, Lina's magnificent lovemaking, and then an outing that had gained her new friends. Either she was in the midst of an incredible stroke of luck, or the dragon-bear had actually mortally wounded her and this was a fever dream before she died.

"Prepare the ship for an overnight in New York," Yvette called out the moment her feet hit the deck. "I've acquired the information we need, and tonight I will investigate our enemy."

"Aye, Captain!" several pirates responded.

Grinning, Yvette bounded toward the stairs, eager to put her new supplies to the test. Lina would be flabbergasted. Which would hopefully lead to more bedsport.

Yvette was mulling over the feasibility of barging into Lina's office fully prepared for a night on the town, when the other woman surprised her instead.

"He took you shopping?"

Lina stood in the doorway to Yvette's cabin, leaning against the jamb as if staking a claim to the place. She glared at the large, rectangular box in Yvette's hands.

"Oui. I did not possess appropriate clothing for this evening's activities. Now I do. I will need help with the corset."

Lina jerked upright. "He bought you *undergarments?*"

Yvette blinked, momentarily at a loss for words. Was Lina scandalized? Lina of many lovers and sex contracts? No. Impossible. But the only other reason to care was… jealousy.

"Yes. All the layers." Yvette smiled sweetly. "Evan is very knowledgeable about women's fashion."

"Evan?" Lina echoed.

Oh, yes. She was jealous. Yvette wanted to dance. No one had ever been jealous over her before. But Lina clearly was. Beautiful, smart, no-nonsense Lina who soothed wounded souls and gave breathtaking orgasms.

Yvette's heart stuttered. This was very, very bad. She was in deep. Too deep to get out, in fact. She hadn't guarded her heart well enough, and she couldn't even regret it. She'd face the inevitable when it happened. Until then, she would take everything she could get.

She nodded toward her cabin. "Step inside and I will explain everything."

Lina's expression remained frosty, but she slipped into the cabin and waited for Yvette to follow before closing the door.

Yvette placed her package on the bed and lifted the top off the box. One-by-one, she removed the layers of gauzy paper to reveal the various items she would use to present herself as an upper-class lady.

"The name of the man who purchased the termites is Pierre Archambeau." Yvette carefully unfolded the delicate overskirt and spread it across her bed. The light in the cabin wasn't good enough to fully display the softness of the fine ivory cotton or the intricacy of the pastel flowers, but in the bright lighting of the opera house, she would shine. "He is a wealthy French merchant who has recently spent much time mingling with New York society."

Lina stepped closer, her gaze sweeping over the clothing. "This is all to allow you to meet him, I assume? I hope you're not going out to dinner posing as Tagget's mistress or some such."

"Don't be silly. Evan is going out dancing with his wife. He's loaned us his private box at the opera. We will observe this Monsieur Archambeau and learn all we can about him and his associates."

Lina's brow furrowed. "We meaning you and I?"

"You have an evening dress, non?"

"Yes."

Of course she did. She came from a fashionable neighborhood in Savannah. She would at least occasionally go to parties. Plus, she surely wanted to flaunt her figure on occasion to seduce the ladies. Yvette tried not to scowl at the thought. Someday Lina would be off seducing new ladies and she would simply have to accept it and move on.

"Good." Yvette resumed arranging the pieces of her opera dress. "You have more experience with fancy events than I do. And you are American, so your accent will not be so memorable if we need to ask questions."

"Anyone will know I'm from the South," Lina argued.

"It is still closer than France."

Lina made a noncommittal noise. "Be honest. You want me to accompany you because you know I'm not the spy."

Yvette froze. The pair of lacy silk stockings she had lifted from the box slipped from her fingers. She spun to face Lina directly.

"No." The thought hadn't even crossed her mind until Lina brought it up. "I want you to accompany me because..."

Because. There wasn't any more to it, really. When Tagget had told Yvette about Archambeau and offered his box, she'd immediately imagined Lina beside her. There'd never been any question in her mind.

"We work well together," she finished, though not until the pause had already grown awkward. "We make a good team."

Lina slowly nodded. "I suppose we do. And someone needs to make sure you keep out of trouble."

Yvette wrinkled her nose. She would be happy to keep out of trouble. If she had her way, she'd be running her usual smuggling routes instead of hunting down enemies with mysterious agendas. Maybe then Lina would stop questioning her every move.

She waved a hand in a dismissive gesture, not bothering to hide her annoyance. If she focused on the annoying things Lina did, it would distract from the silly pitter-pattering in her heart every time she looked at the woman. Maybe it would lessen the future heartbreak.

"You should go dress so we can be sure to be on time," Yvette declared. "I will send one of the crew to assist with your clothing and hair."

Lina cast a long look at Yvette's gown, then dipped her chin in agreement.

· · ● ☕ ● · ·

Lina glared at her own reflection in the mirror. Someone else was lacing Yvette into that pristine white corset, and she had only herself to blame.

Chantal relaxed her grip on Lina's hair. "Did I pull too hard?"

"No. Thinking of other things. You're doing a wonderful job."

Chantal blushed and pinned up another curl. "Thank you."

Lina focused her gaze on the young woman's hands and the practiced way she wielded hairpins. Unfortunately, thinking of hands stirred up memories of Yvette's elegant, clever fingers and the sublime pleasure they could bring.

Lina's jaw tightened, but she managed not to openly scowl again. How the devil was she supposed to behave rationally when her mind was filled with nothing but the vexing pirate captain? Yvette haunted her day and night, like a particularly persistent—but not especially terrifying—ghost. Which left them in real danger of violating their contract.

"You and the captain will look so lovely together." Chantal gave a soft sigh. "It's very romantic, dressing up for a night at the opera."

Lina didn't know if the girl meant romantic in a general sense, or if she was speaking specifically of sapphic love, but either way the damage was done. Lina's heart beat faster and her body tensed with desire. God, how she longed to stride boldly into the opera house with Yvette on her arm. To touch and flirt and perhaps even sneak kisses. To declare to the world, "This woman is *mine*."

She rubbed a thumb over the crack between the tabletop and the drawer beneath. The contract sat at the bottom of that drawer. It would be the work of seconds to pull it out and tear it in half. Or perhaps merely strike out the lines stating that the affair was to be conducted only in private and could not interfere with their work. Those items had seemed reasonable when she'd written them.

They were still reasonable, dammit. She wasn't foolish enough to behave indiscreetly in front of strangers. And while she did know plenty of subtle ways to flirt, this was not a pleasure outing.

"I'm hoping for an opera where the villain gets his due,"

she growled. "I can't wait to put the bastard behind bars. The sooner the better."

Maybe, once they'd defeated their foe, Lina could have Yvette to herself for a few weeks and quench her lust once and for all.

"You are making me jealous." Chantal laughed. "Dressing fancy and hunting scoundrels all at once? It's a wonder every girl does not aspire to the life of a pirate."

"I've never aspired to the life of a pirate."

Lina's own words gave her pause. They were true, yet somehow they rang false in her ears. At this moment, she couldn't imagine herself anywhere else or doing anything different.

She swallowed hard. Was she slipping into her long-ago self, when she'd thought nothing of climbing a ladder to a lover's window in the dead of night, intending to sweep her off her feet and gallop away into the unknown? Impossible. It had to be impossible.

The uncertainty nagged at her throughout the rest of her preparations and as she made her way up to the deck.

Until she spied Yvette.

All other thoughts vanished. The dress had looked pretty spread across the bedsheets. On Yvette, it was mesmerizing. The neckline dipped low, offering a tempting glimpse of her breasts and revealing plenty of creamy skin, even with a lace shawl draped loosely around her shoulders. Lace trim on the sleeves and bodice matched the wrap, and the pops of blue in the printed flowers of the skirt matched her eyes. No extraneous padding or flounces suggested curves she didn't have. Instead, the cut of the gown displayed her lean figure to its best advantage: elegant, graceful, and athletic. Yvette was a woman who could dance the night away and still have stamina for the bedroom afterward.

This time Lina couldn't fault herself for the lurid thought. Because the dress wasn't even the most mesmerizing thing about the lady pirate facing her. Yvette stood proudly with her shoulders back and chest out, one foot forward, as if she might run into Lina's arms at any moment. Her chin was high and her siren's smile could have lured a dozen sailors to their doom. *This is all for you*, the siren song beckoned.

Yvette cocked her hip. "You are beautiful," she stated, as if it were a matter of fact rather than her opinion.

Lina smoothed a hand down her skirt. The pale blue-green gown was simpler than Yvette's, but the color suited Lina's warm skin tone and black hair. "Thank you. You are a vision of loveliness. Where are you hiding your weapons?"

"I'm not telling." Yvette winked and Lina's knees went weak.

This evening was either going to be torture or a hell of a lot of fun.

· · · ☕ · · ·

No one at the opera house would take Yvette for a pirate tonight. Any claim to needing Lina's experience was no more than rubbish. Lina knew Savannah society, and a few rich and notable ladies of lesbian persuasion, but New York boasted elite families of a class she could only imagine. Here in the corridor behind the private boxes, they were surrounded by Vanderbilts, Astors, Goulds, and more. Old money and new. Generations of robber barons. No wonder a professional thief appeared right at home.

Yvette strode down the hall in her usual commanding manner, the perfect picture of a lady with the world at her feet. She didn't gawk, but occasionally nodded appreciatively at the decor. If the other patrons thought her a visitor, they must assume she was accustomed to such luxuries.

Tagget's box was somewhat left of center, though still close enough for an excellent view. A uniformed man stood beside the door. Middle-aged and fit, he wore a sly grin that suggested he'd enjoy throwing out anyone who didn't belong.

"Miss Séverin and Miss Navarro?" he inquired, when Lina and Yvette paused in front of him.

"Oui." Yvette produced a paper from somewhere in her skirts.

The usher glanced at it and nodded. "Enjoy your evening, ladies."

The two women entered the box, and the door clicked closed behind them.

"Séverin?" Lina asked. "Is that your true surname?"

Yvette didn't reply until she had settled herself in one of the front seats. "Oui. From my mother. I would not use my father's family name."

Lina took her seat and adjusted her skirts. "Understandable. I'm only surprised I hadn't heard it sooner. Your crew uses only given names."

"La Liberté is a safe place for women who may not wish their family name known or who might prefer to abandon the name of a cruel husband. No one aboard is ever required to give a surname, so the crew avoids them in most cases."

You called me Miss Navarro.

Had Yvette done that out of respect for Lina as a medical professional, or because she was an outsider? She didn't want to know, so she nodded and said nothing.

Yvette reached beneath her seat, pulled out a small box, and flipped the lid open. "Excellent! They have left us spy glasses."

"Technically, opera glasses are meant for watching the show, not for spying. I'm sure they're not nearly as powerful as anything on your ship."

Yvette smirked and peered through the glasses. They were elegant, but understated, mostly black with narrow gold trim. Tagget's personal pair, most likely.

"Oh." Lina fumbled beneath her own seat, finding another box. The glasses inside were white and decorated with violets.

A small brass slider rested next to the standard focus wheel. "I suppose I ought to consider the source of these devices."

A quick check confirmed that the opera glasses were modified for spying, but Lina didn't bother to waste her time scanning the crowd. Watching Yvette provided vastly better entertainment.

The pirate's mouth was set in a line of concentration, the same expression she wore when flying the ship. She made a thorough perusal of the theater, taking in everything from the stage to the balconies, giving anyone looking the impression of a curious, but harmless, observer.

Lina leaned close, as if to speak confidentially. Yvette smelled of fragrant wood and delicate blossoms. The diamonds dangling from her earlobe caught the light. Lina closed her eyes, visualizing what might happen if she slowly slid that earring away and put her tongue to the spot instead. Lord Almighty.

"The competence with which you make mischief never ceases to amaze me." Lina let her breath skate across Yvette's neck as she spoke. "Do you have any idea how arousing it is?"

The opera glasses wobbled in Yvette's hand.

"Hurry up and find this bastard so we can get back to the ship. I want to peel that dress off you."

Lina straightened up. This was only bending the rules. She was encouraging work, not interfering with it.

Why don't you tell me why you really want to break the rules, Catalina?

Yvette's hand brushed Lina's thigh, silencing her nagging inner therapist. The pirate captain tapped a single finger against the opera glasses Lina had dropped in her lap.

"You wish to go to bed? Help me look for Archambeau. He is a tall white man, blond with a touch of gray. Evan called him, 'damned alluring—in an evil henchman sort of way.' I don't know who he will be with tonight, but he can be identified by the jeweled bird he always wears."

Lina picked up the glasses. "Blond with a bird. I'm afraid 'alluring' isn't a help, as I don't find any men alluring."

"I never understand this." Yvette shook her head. "People of all types can be alluring to me."

Lina pointed her spy glasses at the boxes across the theater, using the magnifying slider to take closer looks at any blond men. "Well, we all like different foods, different colors, different clothing. Naturally, we all have different taste in people, too."

"Oui. But it still confuses my brain. I think some people may be sad because I have more choices of romantic partners."

Lina's grip tightened on the glasses. "I don't care how many choices you have as long as I'm the one who gets to have you."

She nearly clapped a hand over her own mouth. True, she loathed the idea of Yvette with any other romantic partners. But to succumb to irrational jealousy?

A clear sign of infatuation, her inner voice mocked her.

"Very romantic," Yvette replied approvingly. "Will you duel any rivals? I would like to see you with a sword in your hand. Perhaps I will ask Zahra to give you—"

She broke off so suddenly that Lina spun in her seat to face her. "What is it? Did you find Archambeau?"

"Vautour," Yvette spat, her expression contorting in fury.

"What does that mean? Is it a French curse word?"

Yvette's laugh was abrupt and mirthless. "No." She lowered the opera glasses, but her gaze remained fixed on whatever she'd discovered. "It's a name. When I knew this 'Archambeau,' he went by Vautour. He was my father's chief assassin."

24

YVETTE CROSSED HER LEGS, uncrossed them, then crossed them in the opposite direction. No good. No matter how she sat, she couldn't feel comfortable.

She settled for the more ladylike position of crossing her legs at the ankle, then adjusted her skirts. Again. At this rate, the fabric would be a wrinkled mess by the end of Act One.

Lina sat tensely in the next seat over. Probably fighting the urge to snap at Yvette for the constant fidgeting. Yvette didn't dare look her in the eye. A look of disapproval would break her heart. Just once, she wanted to pretend she could be more than a source of frustration and disappointment.

She peered through Evan's delightful spy glasses at the scene onstage. A handsome, talented couple were singing a passionate love ballad. At any other time, she would get lost in the music and emotion, eager to see how the story played out.

Unless this was a tragedy. If so, she needed to leave before the end. She wasn't in the mood for anything but happy endings.

Regardless, any chance at enjoyment had been ruined by the sight of that bastard Vautour. How she'd hoped he'd been part of her father's last mission, dead on a mountainside to be picked at by the vultures he was named for.

"Are you going to tell me more about this assassin?" Lina whispered. "Because from the way you're acting, I'd reckon he's bad news."

Yvette adjusted her position yet again. "He is the cleverest and most malevolent of all my father's henchmen. He uses his handsome face and charming manners to get close to people. Then he murders, seduces, steals, blackmails, or whatever other nasty thing he thinks will benefit him." She hesitated a moment, then shrugged. Lina ought to know the rest, embarrassing though it was. "He toyed with my affections when I was only fifteen. Of all the people I knew, he was the kindest to me. He told me I was clever and beautiful. He brought me little gifts of sweets, saying I deserved all the nicest things and that men ought to fall at my feet. It went on until I was mad in love with him. Then, when he tired of the game, he taunted me over how naive and silly I was. I'm sure the only reason he refrained from doing me any physical harm was to avoid my father's wrath. Plenty of other people were not so fortunate."

Lina made a noise that sounded almost like a growl. "Do we get to kill him? He sounds like he needs killing."

Yvette turned sharply. Kill him? When had proper, prudent Lina become a proper pirate? There went any last hope of not falling in love. Vengeful pirate Lina was the sexiest woman Yvette had ever seen. The sexiest woman she could imagine, in fact. Why were they in this public place wearing all these ridiculous layers, when they could be at home in bed declaring undying devotion?

Vautour. That fils de pute.

"He does need killing," Yvette agreed. "But first, we need to learn more about his plans. We must watch where he goes in the intermission and spy on him."

Lina's feral smile made Yvette's blood heat. "I will be happy to assist."

"Thank you."

"And know this." Lina's expression softened. "He may have

been cruel, but he did speak some truths." She touched the tips of her fingers to Yvette's arm. "You *are* clever and beautiful. And you absolutely deserve all the nicest things."

Yvette's pulse went wild. She shook off her shawl to cool her skin. If Lina didn't stop touching her, she might swoon, and then she'd never be able to show her face in front of her crew again. Pirates didn't swoon.

She winced. *Pirates also don't fall hopelessly in love with ladies they can't have.*

Yvette took the only escape she could think of. She fumbled for the opera glasses, watched Vautour, and contemplated ways to destroy him.

Intermission came mercifully soon. The moment Vautour exited his box, Lina and Yvette sprang to their feet. Yvette pushed aside the curtain and opened the door at the back of the box. She motioned for Lina to step out first.

"I cannot let Vautour see me, or we will lose our chance to learn anything. Even in these clothes, he is certain to recognize me. I will approach him from behind, but you may need to be the one to get close and listen."

"I'll do my best."

Yvette gave Lina a playful nudge. "Not your worst?"

"I save that for the ladies," Lina purred, then sauntered off down the hall.

Yvette followed behind her taller companion, peering around her now and again in search of their enemy. The hunt didn't take long. Monsieur Pierre Archambeau was here to see and be seen. He stood in the center of a large foyer that adjoined the main corridor, chatting and drinking with a group of men. All through the space, other fashionable people did the same thing.

Yvette met Lina's gaze. They exchanged a nod of understanding, then separated and moved in to flank their opponent.

Yvette wafted through the foyer, casting flirtatious smiles

at the men she passed. When they smiled back, she batted her eyelashes. It didn't matter whether they thought her a husband-hunting debutante or a courtesan. They would see a shallow, coquettish girl. Definitely not a pirate or spy.

A trio of women playing coy for their own reasons gave Yvette her opportunity. They had cornered a handsome young man, backing him into eavesdropping distance of Vautour's cluster. The man was grinning like a child with stolen candy, eyeing each lady in turn. Yvette stared directly at him as she approached, and when she caught his eye she flashed the kind of smile she wanted to give Lina.

He winked at her. "So many lovely ladies here tonight!"

Yvette sidled up to him. "Merci, Monsieur. How charming you Americans are."

"I try, mademoiselle. But truly, it is I who must thank you." He waved a hand to indicate all the ladies. "I can't think of a better way to spend an evening than surrounded by such beauty."

Yvette tilted her head, fanned her lashes, and ceased to pay him any further attention.

Vautour stood close enough that she could pick out his French accent among the other voices. As she listened, she kept her hands busy, playing with her hair or picking at a thread on her bodice to continue the ruse of flirtation. Phrases such as "make arrangements" and "exclusive deal" jumped out at her. They could have been part of any business discussion, but given Vautour's history, he was almost certainly fishing for buyers of smuggled goods. And perhaps even business of a more nefarious kind.

"Something subtle," said the American directly facing Vautour—and therefore Yvette. "Can't have monster dragons destroying things all higgledy-piggledy and making the papers."

"Did you see that bat-girl, though?" exclaimed another, so loudly that Yvette didn't need to strain to hear. "She saved the city, they're saying. Thwarted the enemies of democracy! Gave the beast a good ol' New York welcome!"

Yvette beamed. Oh, what she wouldn't give to see Vautour's face. He was probably grinding his teeth to nubs, trying to keep from openly scowling.

"Filthy pirates," Vautour snarled, as if he weren't one himself. "They must have sent the dragon. How could one small woman destroy such a creature unless it was her own device?"

Yvette muttered a curse. How dare that bastard both blame her and insult her!

"Beg pardon, mademoiselle?" her flirtatious decoy asked.

"A French compliment." The idea of him repeating the phrase and mistakenly swearing at someone was enough to restore Yvette's smile. She plucked the flower from his lapel and held it to her nose to cover any further accidental displays of displeasure.

Vautour's group hadn't stopped discussing the bear-dragon attack. The loud man was defending her, sounding almost rapturous when he called her an avenging angel. He was now her favorite American—after Lina and Nora and Evan.

Vautour had begun grumbling, making his words harder to distinguish, but Yvette guessed he was attempting to steer the conversation back to business. The others talked over him, until he raised his voice.

"We cannot trust that a flying girl will always appear and take a lucky shot," he declared. "I believe we need a strong leader to defend against future attacks. An international security force, led by someone with the skills and resources to stop monster machines before they can destroy a city."

Curse the man! He was seeking investors, not buyers. People to help him fund a private army. And if Yvette and her crew were standing in the way of that, they would be target number one.

She'd heard enough. She craned her neck, trying to spot Lina through the crowd of men.

"Mademoiselle? Do you find me tedious?" The flirt made puppy-dog eyes at her. Damn. She'd forgotten to keep playing the coquette.

Yvette opened her mouth to blurt an apology, but he spun around abruptly to see who she was looking at.

"Who are you—" He crashed into Vautour, sending him staggering forward. "Oh! I'm so sorry!"

Vautour caught his balance and started to turn.

Yvette ran.

25

LINA WORMED HER WAY through the crowd, trying to reach Yvette before everything went to hell. The pirate assassin—Vautour or Archambeau or whatever his real name was—hadn't turned fully around before he'd been intercepted by the apologizing dandy who'd bumped him. But that didn't mean he hadn't seen and recognized Yvette. Time to retreat and regroup.

Lina caught a flash of blond hair and white lace disappearing through the opening to the main corridor and rushed to follow. The moment she stepped out of the foyer, a hand seized her arm.

"Is he coming?" Yvette hissed. Her gaze darted in the direction of their seats, then back to Lina.

"I don't know."

A door a few boxes down banged open, and they both jumped. A server carrying a tray of empty champagne flutes stepped out. As he turned away, Yvette hauled Lina toward the open door. The pirate jammed her foot into the opening in time to prevent the door closing, then slipped inside, pulling Lina after her.

The door clicked closed behind them. Only a narrow beam of light from beyond the curtain kept the small passageway from total blackness. Laughter and trilling voices sounded from the box—at least three people that Lina could distinguish.

The hot caress of Yvette's breath tickled Lina's ear. "We will remain here until the opera resumes."

Lina nodded, though she wasn't certain how well Yvette could see. Her own eyes began to adjust, revealing the outline of several cloaks hung beside her. She nudged Yvette toward the wall. The hanging garments would provide a small amount of concealment, if anyone happened to peek behind the curtain.

As they settled into place, Yvette's arm brushed against Lina's, bare skin to bare skin. The temperature in the chamber seemed to jump ten degrees. She was huddled in the dark with the lover she wasn't supposed to be touching, hiding from a killer pirate, and in danger of being discovered at any moment.

And it thrilled her. Her body burned with lust and energy, every sense on high alert, her mind racing with the possibilities.

She stiffened. Yvette had been right. So had the irritating voice in the back of her mind. She hadn't grown out of her childhood longing for adventure; she'd simply repressed it. Life in Savannah had been comfortable, but it had become stale, repetitive. A part of her had needed to see the world, try new things, and discover who Catalina Navarro really was.

That particular discovery remained incomplete. At the moment, however, Catalina Navarro was a woman giving herself the freedom to enjoy illicit adventures with a sexy pirate.

Muffled sounds of voices and footsteps carried through the door as people made their way along the main corridor to and from their seats. They had some time left to wait. The bell hadn't yet rung to alert the audience that the show would restart soon.

Her brain, funny thing that it was, began to play tricks on her. Outside her hiding place, the world moved on as normal, but here, time seemed to have come to a standstill. No change. No movement. Only the repetition of her breathing and her heartbeat.

Yvette began to fidget.

Lina didn't blame her. Holding still was unnatural to her. Her body operated best when in motion. And she couldn't know that her every twitch felt to Lina like a seductive caress.

Oh, to hell with it.

Lina turned and brushed her lips against Yvette's shoulder. They may as well occupy their minds and their bodies, since the alternative was agonized waiting.

"You are—" Yvette's whisper turned into a gasp when Lina's kisses inched lower. "Breaking the rules."

"I am providing an occupation until we are free to leave."

This flimsy excuse apparently satisfied Yvette, because she pushed aside her shawl to expose more skin.

Lina moved slowly, savoring each taste. As her lips crept down, her hands slid up, her fingers light against the soft fabric of Yvette's evening gown. Lord, she was beautiful, even in the dark. Every bit of her was perfection, from the subtle flare of her hips to the upthrust mounds of her breasts.

Lina had barely begun to explore that well-presented bosom, when the bell sounded. Just her luck.

Yvette scooted closer to the door, pressing her ear against it. Lina held still, listening intently.

The noise in the corridor swelled. Doors opened and closed. Voices rose and fell as people passed by. Again, time seemed to crawl. The rush continued. If Lina hadn't known better, she would have sworn every single person in the theater was walking by this one box.

She blew out a long breath when the sounds at last began to fade. Their time in hiding was almost up. Which also meant her time for clandestine groping was up. Damn.

The house lights dimmed, until Lina couldn't even see her hand in front of her face. Orchestral music filled the air. On to Act Two.

"We wait a few minutes," Yvette murmured. "Then we go quietly."

A few minutes which they would spend alone in the dark. Lina caught her lover around the waist and resumed her amorous ministrations. Now that listening was no longer of utmost importance, Yvette began explorations of her own, caressing Lina through the fine fabric of her shawl and mussing her neatly coiffed hair.

So much clothing. Lina liked her dress. She liked Yvette's. But the longer this went on, the more she yearned to rip both garments apart and free the bodies underneath. They needed to go home, where they could finish this the right way.

She disentangled herself from Yvette, knocking down one of the hanging cloaks in the process. No matter. Concealment wouldn't matter anymore.

"Should we go?" she whispered.

Please say yes. This corset is strangling me, and I don't even tight-lace.

Yvette didn't reply, but her skirts rustled. Was she nodding enthusiastically? Reaching for the door? Or was she shaking her head emphatically?

Lina closed the space between them again. Perhaps her hushed words had been too indistinct to hear. Her lips had just grazed Yvette's ear, when the door swung open.

Light flooded the space as they sprang apart. Lina squinted at the silhouette of a man standing in the entranceway. His features came gradually into focus. Dark suit. Blond hair. And a knife at the ready.

"I knew you were hiding somewhere, Little Sister," the pirate sneered.

Lina seized the nearest cloak and hurled it at him, then grabbed Yvette's wrist and dragged her through the curtain.

The ladies in the box shrieked in outraged terror at this invasion of their space. One flung her champagne glass, but it sailed past Lina and Yvette and smashed on the floor.

Lina hiked up her skirts and swung a leg over the

decorative rail that separated one box from the next. "I do beg your pardon, ladies."

Yvette followed, putting a hand to Lina's back to urge her faster. "Allez!"

Lina pushed past the occupants of the next box and again hopped the rail. Yvette darted past her, traipsing across the front wall of the box like an acrobat.

"Get down from there before you fall!" Lina blurted, but her words were swallowed up by a dozen other voices shouting about the scene now unfolding.

"Stop them!" Archambeau roared.

Yvette hopped down into the next box, reaching out a hand to help Lina along. A man snatched at her arm, but Yvette shoved him right into the lap of one of his companions. More shouts arose, not only from the nearby boxes but from all across the theater. On stage, the performers tried valiantly to carry on.

Lina jumped another rail, starting to feel the rhythm of the movement. Yvette was still faster and more nimble, but Lina didn't slow her down enough for their enemy to catch up, which was all that mattered. Five more boxes and they could drop safely onto the stage and escape through the back of the theater. Thank God she'd worn sensible flat slippers tonight.

"Stop them!" Archambeau's voice sounded more distant, but Lina didn't dare turn back. "Stop those thieves!"

Two men in the box ahead shoved chairs out of the way and braced themselves, eyes gleaming at the prospect of grappling villainous women. Yvette again hopped up onto the front wall of the box and skittered past, but Lina didn't dare attempt such a feat. She froze, straddling the divider rail.

Back, bad. Forward, bad.

Her heart pounded. One of the men made a grab for her. "Yvette!"

The pirate captain rose up behind the men, grabbed fistfuls of their hair, and smashed their heads together. Both men staggered, and Lina darted between them.

"Thank you."

"A pleasure, ma belle."

Yvette took hold of Lina's hand, and they climbed together into the next—thankfully empty—box.

By now the entire theater was in an uproar. Among the shouts of the throng were numerous calls to "stop the show" and "turn on the lights!"

And then, "The bat girl!"

A second voice took up the cry. "That's the bat girl! The girl who killed the monster!"

Bat girl. Flying girl. Dragon slayer. The words traveled around the theater as Lina and Yvette scampered through the last few boxes. Yvette appeared entirely undaunted by the shouting and pointing, but surely it affected her on some level. Or would, when she had time to stop and think.

The people in the two boxes nearest the stage let them through without a fight. Yvette swung herself over the edge of the last box and easily shimmied down the relief carving decorating the wall at the very corner of the stage.

Lina lowered herself gingerly. Already her hands were slippery with sweat from the exertion, and she didn't want to tumble and hurt herself or ruin the escape. Foot, hand. Foot, hand. One limb at a time, creeping downward.

Halfway down, a steadying hand touched the back of her leg.

"One more step, then jump," Yvette urged. "I have you."

Lina slid lower, poking around with her toe until she found a foothold. She took a deep breath, then jumped. Yvette caught her arm, guiding her to the ground. Lina landed with only a slight stumble. She'd made it.

"We did it!"

Lina looked up and then cursed herself for having spoken too soon. The opera had ceased entirely, and a crowd of furious actors was bearing down on her.

Without a word, Lina and Yvette clasped hands and

bolted. They dodged actors and crew, and shoved aside props, caring nothing for the mess or the noise they made. Only two things mattered. Stay together. Get out.

A large sign reading "7th Avenue Exit" marked the back door. A scowling security guard stepped in front of it, blocking their path with his large, muscled frame.

Lina skittered to a halt.

Yvette, however, kept going. She released Lina, plunged her hand into her skirts, and yanked something out. Was that… perfume?

Yvette raised the bottle as she ran straight at the guard. At the last moment, she changed direction, neatly sidestepping his grasping hands. She gave the atomizer a firm squeeze, hitting the man in the face with a cloud of mist.

The guard choked and staggered. Lina rushed him, shoving him aside while Yvette reached for the door handle. The scent of cedar and citrus tickled Lina's nose. A rush of cool air blew through the open door.

The two women clasped hands again and darted out into the night. They raced down the street, frantically waving at every cab that rumbled by. Three blocks later, one finally stopped.

They scrambled inside, and Yvette tossed the driver a coin before Lina could even get the door closed behind her.

"The airfield. Quickly."

The steam engine chugged, and the car rolled off, slipping away into the New York traffic.

Yvette closed the panel separating the driver and passenger compartments. Lina slumped against the seat back, letting her heart rate and breathing slow to normal. What a ride. What an adventure!

A laugh burst out of her. Then another. In moments, she was clutching her side, tears streaming down her cheeks.

"That was…" she gasped between peals of laughter. "The most ridiculous thing… I have ever done!"

Yvette did not join in the merriment. When Lina recovered herself, she glanced up to find the pirate appraising her with a slight frown.

"Is that a good thing?" Yvette wondered. "Or bad?"

"I don't know," Lina answered honestly.

But she knew one thing. If Yvette asked her to do it all over again, she would say yes.

26

BAT-GIRL CHAOS AT THE MET

Last night's performance at the Metropolitan Opera House brought the audience to its feet, but not for the usual reasons. Early in Act Two, a pair of women barged into a private box, after which they proceeded to scamper from one box to the next in a fashion so shocking that ladies swooned and gentlemen were rendered speechless. It is reported that this pair of hoydens left broken glass and splintered wood in their wake, as well as causing severe distress and injury to more than one party.

This writer was unable to confirm the identity of either woman, however, numerous eye-witnesses testified that one of them appeared to be the very same "Bat-Girl" who in a stunning spectacle destroyed the ursine dragon attacking the Waldorf-Astoria hotel.

"I would hate to speculate," said Mr. Pierre Archambeau, a visiting businessman who sounded the alarm when the pair of thieves absconded with his billfold, "but the blond woman seemed familiar."

If she is indeed the daring maiden who swooped in to save the city, what possible motive could she have for public criminal shenanigans? Might we suppose the dragon battle was not what it seemed? Perhaps the perpetrator of this operatic pandemonium thrives on spectacle and courts infamy. Or mayhap she harbors a distaste for Manhattan's finest establishments.

Hero or villain? Friend or foe? The investigation is ongoing.

*Y*VETTE HANDED THE NEWSPAPER to Kaina, then picked up her spoon and returned to her boiled egg. She was a lady. She was a captain. She would not disrupt breakfast with a furious tirade in front of the crew.

The dread pirate Redbeard plots her revenge in a calm and calculated manner. She is not emotional and impulsive.

Yvette forced herself to swallow a bite of egg. If she kept telling herself these things, perhaps they would become the truth.

"What a horrible man!" Kaina exclaimed. She passed the paper to Esme. "I am certain this is all his doing."

"Bastard," Esme agreed, as her eyes scanned the article. "'Hate to speculate,' my arse. He's intentionally throwing the blame on the captain."

The newspaper continued around the table, earning more grumbles and curses.

Yvette set down her spoon and addressed her crew. "We must leave New York today. I will not wait for trouble when there is no more to learn here. Vautour's identity tells us enough. He isn't a man who builds intricate machines." Most of the pirates wouldn't need this explanation, but Lina and the twins weren't familiar with the old Redbeard's crew, and Yvette didn't want anyone left out. "But he would use them. I assume he possesses my father's large cargo ships."

Probably most of his fortune, too. She had seized and sold a few smaller ships and emptied one bank account, but everything else had been looted before she got to it.

"So he's buying mechanical monsters from that school?" Lina asked.

"Allies rather than buyer and seller, I think," Kaina surmised. "Headmistress von Arx at the Institute leads the Daughters of Redbeard and Vautour leads the pirate men, but they share a single plan."

Yvette nodded. "I agree. We must return to Europe, restock our supplies, and make a plan."

Paris. They needed to start in Paris, where she had contacts and informants. The whole crew would know this once they set their course. And yet the exact destination stuck in her throat. She hadn't resolved the matter of the spy. Beneath the table, she tapped her foot in relentless agitation.

Zahra waved the newspaper. "Do we find a journalist and return the favor before we go?"

"Yes," Olga agreed. "But not if it takes so long that someone comes for the captain."

Heads nodded all around.

"The captain's safety first," Angelique declared. "Then, vengeance."

"Vengeance!" the crew echoed.

Lina raised her teacup in salute, and the pirates joined her, filling the air with the dainty clinks of elegant porcelain.

Yvette's gaze swept up and down the table, lingering on each face in turn. There couldn't be a spy here. These women were fiercely loyal. They were good people. Good friends.

Moisture gathered in the corners of her eyes. Her crew cared for her. She cared for them in return. The thought of betrayal had been eating away at her. And it would only keep hurting as long as she fought what her gut had been telling her all along: she could trust them.

"We'll go to Paris," she blurted. "We can get everything we need there. Kaina, I'll need you to write up the supplies list. We want to be prepared as soon as possible. We are taking the fight to our enemy. Everyone who spent time at the Illyrian

Institute, we will need maps, schedules, security information, or anything else that might help us. We're storming the castle and destroying the machines. Destroying all the tools they need to make more. Then, with the machines gone, we go after Vautour."

"Chantal is good at drawing and I have a good memory," Clara spoke up. "We can make the map."

Zahra tapped her chin thoughtfully. "If you can finish it in a day or two, we can have a plan of attack prepared by the time we reach Paris. Brigid, can you add any hidden passages and rooms you know to the map?"

Instead of Brigid's usual brisk reply, the question was met with silence.

Yvette's gaze snapped to Brigid. Her face had gone pale and she sat with her head down and shoulders hunched. "What's wrong?"

"M-meine Schwester."

It took a moment for Yvette to realize that Brigid was referring to an actual blood sibling. Years of the Daughters of Redbeard calling one another "sister" had muddled the term in her mind, especially when someone said it in a language other than French.

"Your older sister is a teacher at the Institute?" Yvette hoped she remembered that correctly. "She will come to no harm. This Redbeard does not attack innocents. The mission is to destroy their operations, not to kill anyone. Unless we must defend ourselves, of course."

Brigid pushed her chair back from the table, shaking her head. "I must tell her. I must send her a wire so she can prepare. She cannot be there if something goes wrong."

"No." Yvette popped up from her seat and planted her hand firmly on the table. "No telegrams. Von Arx will intercept them and we will lose the chance for a surprise attack."

"But..." Brigid squeaked.

An uneasy silence fell over the room. Several pirates shifted in their seats. A few looked up at Yvette with wide, sad eyes. What was this? True, it was unusual for her to so firmly deny a request, but it wasn't unheard of. It was her responsibility to make decisions for the good of the whole crew.

"Brigid always sends telegrams." Angelique's soft voice almost echoed in the stillness. "It might appear suspicious if she doesn't."

Yvette's heart skipped a beat. Beside her, Lina inhaled sharply.

Telegrams. Suspicious.

Putain! Every airfield had a telegraph office. And she'd never forbidden the crew from leaving the ship or writing letters. Brigid probably hadn't given the matter a second thought. How long had someone from the Institute been reading her correspondence and passing the information on to Vautour?

By the looks of sorrow on the pirates' faces, they all realized the source of the leak. Kaina and Esme clasped hands for support. Not one person scowled or accused. Zahra, seated next to Brigid, turned toward her to offer comfort.

Brigid shied away. Her jaw trembled as if she might cry. "W-wir schreiben immer verschlüsselt!"

"You always write in code?" Yvette translated, mostly for Lina's benefit. "But not La Capitaine's unbreakable code."

"N-nein. Wir haben keine Maschine." Tears began to pour down Brigid's cheeks. "Ich bin n-nicht eine Spionin!"

No, she wasn't a spy. She was a young woman afraid of losing contact with the only family she had. La Liberté was supposed to be a place where the crew could belong. Where no woman was left behind. Yet Brigid looked so heartbreakingly alone.

She dashed the tears from her eyes and rose from her seat. "I will pack my things," she said in English. "I will go quick."

"We are *not* leaving you," Yvette snapped.

Brigid flinched, then her brow furrowed.

"You made a mistake," Yvette continued. "But we do not punish mistakes on this ship. That is the old Redbeard way."

Lina reached out as if to take Yvette's hand. Yvette quickly stuffed her hands in her pockets to avoid the temptation. What was Lina thinking? Did she want to violate the contract? Hadn't they stretched the rules far enough last night?

Lina let her hand drop. "And the new Redbeard way?" she prompted.

"We help each other. We learn. We fix things." Yvette looked directly at Brigid. "You will correct your mistake by using your telegrams to fight our enemies. And we will protect your sister. *That* is the new Redbeard way." She gestured at the door. "Everyone on takeoff duty come with me. Everyone else has galley cleanup. We fly!"

"Aye, Captain!" the crew chorused. Chairs scraped across the floor as everyone sprang into action at once.

Lina caught Yvette's arm before she could walk away. "A moment, Captain?"

Yvette allowed Lina to steer her into the corner of the room. This didn't seem to be a romantic proposition, but her body thrilled to the touch regardless. She took a moment to savor the sensation of Lina's warm hand and soft smile. These memories would be all that remained after Lina's inevitable departure. That meant storing them up and treasuring them for the future.

"Do you have a question, Catalina?"

"No." Lina's voice was barely more than a whisper. "I only wanted to say how impressed I was with the way you handled that situation. You were strong, sensible, and compassionate. You are a true leader and I think this crew would walk through fire for you. *That* is the Captain Yvette Séverin way." She gave a nod of approval, then walked off to join the cleanup crew.

For a moment, Yvette couldn't move, frozen in place by the most beautiful compliment anyone had ever given her. Maybe

Lina would never love her the way she longed for, but Lina believed in her. Respected her.

Eventually her body broke free from the trance and she scampered up to the deck. Her stride never faltered as she ascended to the bridge, but she kept her gaze straight ahead at all times. She couldn't speak. Couldn't look at anyone. If she heard another kind word or caught even a glimpse of a fond smile, it would wreck her. Already she feared her heart might burst from the deluge of emotions. At the helm, she would have work to focus on. And she could pass off any tears as the sting of the wind.

The dread pirate Redbeard is calm, not emotional. She does not...

But, no. That wasn't right. She *was* emotional. And impulsive. She had a heart and people she loved, and she wasn't afraid to make snap decisions to protect those people. She could plan and plot, but it was always her instincts that served her best. Instincts that had told her no one here would truly betray her. Instincts that had allowed her to defeat the dragon-bear. Even the idea to bring Lina on board had been one of those lightning-quick decisions.

The dread pirate Yvette is a good captain. Just as she is.

When her hands gripped the wheel, she let the tears flow and her heart soar.

27

$\mathcal{L}$INA HAD NEVER SEEN all the pirates out of uniform at once before. Plain, muted fabrics replaced the vibrant blues and crisp whites that usually brightened the ship. Today was a day for blending in. The women would vanish into the Paris crowds, no different than all the others out for their daily trips to the market.

"Angelique and Olga," Kaina announced.

The two women stepped forward and Kaina handed them a list.

"Memorize it, then destroy it," the purser instructed. "And stay together. The captain doesn't want anyone alone." She glanced down at her next paper. "Clara and Chantal."

"On our own?" Chantal gasped.

Kaina gave the girls a wide smile. "The captain thinks you're ready. I didn't put weapons or anything unusual on your list, so this should be a straightforward assignment."

The twins shared a look, then nodded in unison and went to claim their paper.

Lina glanced at Yvette, who stood off to the side, observing the proceedings. She bounced in her usual energetic manner, smiling fondly at her crew.

Despite the seriousness of this undertaking, Yvette's mood

had been light throughout the cross-Atlantic journey. She'd overseen the planning with constant enthusiasm and lured Lina to her bed every night with teasing touches and flirtatious words.

Lina had no cause for complaint, but she did have to wonder what had caused the abundance of good cheer.

"Brigid and Zahra, you have a short list because your first priority is the telegram with the false directions," Kaina continued. "Memorize the list, destroy it, stay together." She waved a final piece of paper. "Esme and I will stay to guard the ship, then gather the remaining supplies when the first group returns."

Esme jogged to Kaina's side, leaving Lina standing alone, unpartnered and without an assignment. All around her, the pairs pored over their lists, seemingly oblivious to this oversight.

"Do I not have a task?" Lina asked. Dammit, was she still not a part of the crew after all this time? She'd lived through adventures and participated in the planning for this mission. Why would they leave her out?

Kaina cocked her head, frowning in obvious confusion. "You're with the captain."

Lina's lips parted in a little O of surprise, and she rushed to compose herself. "Yes. That's fine."

Yvette wasn't part of the supply run. As captain, she had the task of seeking out and hiring a ship to serve as an evacuation vessel for Brigid's sister and any other teachers and students at the school who were not a part of the headmistress's schemes. Lina hadn't the first idea how to hire a ship or choose someone reliable. She didn't know the city, and her grasp of French remained limited to food words and simple greetings. Yet the crew had apparently assumed she would be Yvette's second in this matter.

Esme gave Lina a wink. "We trust you not to distract each other too much."

A pang of guilt knotted Lina's stomach. *If you only knew what happened in the dark at the opera...*

"Fine," Lina said again. "Fine."

Ugh. She sounded like a ninny instead of a mature, worldly woman. Before anything else foolish could spill from her lips, she sauntered to Yvette's side and adopted an air of insouciance.

"I suppose someone has to keep an eye on you."

Yvette ran her hands down her red captain's coat. "I *am* very pretty to look at."

Lina couldn't disagree. That coquettish smirk. The jut of her hip. The gleam in her dazzling eyes. Lina could look all day and still not get enough. A distraction indeed.

"Is there anything that needs doing before we set out?" she asked.

Yvette's expression sobered. "No. The ship is secure and I have everything I need. We're not going far. The ships-for-hire moor at the east end of the airfield."

Lina used the sun to orient herself. "Not far" was a relative term, it seemed. La Liberté had landed near the northwest corner of the airfield, and it had to be a mile or more from one end to the other. A long way to walk in a conspicuous red coat.

Lina ran a finger over one of the decorative clasps of her corset. One firm twist of the bottom clasp would release the slim blade hidden in the busk. Several of her corsets had hidden knives, but this garment—a deep gold brocade that matched the subtle pinstriping in her charcoal split skirt—made the weapon particularly easy to access. She didn't know how to hire a ship, but she could help keep Yvette safe.

They were the first of the crew to disembark, Yvette leading the way with easy, confident strides. Despite their previous troubles in Paris and the possibility of enemies searching for her, it was clear she felt at home here. Lina had to walk quickly to match her stride.

"Am I the only one who doesn't know this city?" she asked.

Yvette spread her hands in her French shrug.

"It's an excuse to pair me with you, if a flimsy one." Lina sighed. "Though excuses seem silly now. It's clear the whole crew knows about us."

"Et alors?"

"So… the public flirtation and affection clause seems unnecessary."

It felt good to finally say it. That damnable contract had been bothering her for days, if not weeks. Why shouldn't they flirt whenever the mood struck them? Why not share an embrace in front of their friends? Yvette was a spontaneous, free-spirited woman. It was wrong to box her in with rules and timelines. Lina was of a mind to pitch the whole contract into the fire.

"It all seems unnecessary," she added. "We can do away with it, if you like."

Yvette spun to look at Lina, and for the tiniest fraction of a second, excitement flashed in her eyes. Then it was gone, replaced with a grim determination.

"No. I'm not interested in changing things. It's nice how it is. We can manage until you leave."

The words stung like a slap. Yvette may as well have said, "I'm bored with you. Goodbye."

This wasn't the first hint, either. Several times during their recent voyage Yvette had uttered phrases like, "when you're back home," or, "after this is finished." She viewed their time together as finite and their separation as not only given, but imminent.

And I… don't.

The thought was odd. She'd always been content with temporary relationships. But Yvette made temporary seem wrong. Yvette made Lina want to claim her, like some overbearing medieval lord swearing to fight off any challengers.

Again, Lina touched a clasp on her corset. *Protect her. Make her happy. Never let her go.*

Fuck. She was well and truly infatuated.

"You are frowning," Yvette observed. Uncertainty shadowed her face and her stride had become uncharacteristically slow. "Why don't you like the contract anymore?"

"It's fine," Lina said hurriedly. Lord Almighty, she wished she could expunge that word from her vocabulary. "I just thought you might… prefer something different."

"Non." Yvette turned her attention back to the airfield and resumed her usual pace.

Lina trailed along, trying not to stomp. All the psychological studies in the world couldn't help her understand everyone at all times. Hell, she didn't entirely understand herself. Right now, Yvette seemed the most mystifying of all.

She was so passionate, in and out of bed. At night she cuddled close, her face radiant with happiness, as if Lina's arms provided perfect comfort. Yet she resisted changing the contract. She hid her true feelings behind her captain's mask, and Lina couldn't discern whether those feelings were good, bad, or simply indifferent. Not when the fog of her own muddled wants and fears was so thick.

They lapsed into silence for a time, until Yvette began to point out examples of ships that didn't suit her purposes. Too big, too small, in bad repair, too opulent, too slow, too unwieldy for mountain navigation—the list went on and on. Even after all her time on La Liberté, Lina's knowledge of airships was too limited to see many of the flaws Yvette did. The longer they walked, the more she feared they might not find any ship at all.

"What if none are suitable?" she asked.

Yvette shrugged again. "The captain is the most important part. A ship that isn't perfect but has a skilled and trustworthy captain is better than a perfect ship with a bad captain."

"An excellent point. Do you know some of these captains-for-hire by reputation? Should I expect a lengthy interv—"

"Ah!" Yvette jumped in excitement. "Your question is unnecessary. The perfect ship is here! Come. Quickly. Before someone else can hire her." She broke into energetic, bouncing steps that nearly veered into skipping.

Lina jogged to keep up, only slowing when their destination became clear. Directly ahead stood a long, sleek ship, painted in tidy blue and white. Red stenciled letters declared, "Expéditions de Luxe."

"Is this a charter ship?" she called to Yvette. "For explorers or adventurers?"

The pirate glanced over her shoulder and flashed a wide grin. "C'est ça. Her captain was once part of Sabine's crew. Now she carries passengers to remote or dangerous locations." Yvette slowed her steps to a professional swagger. "Come. I will introduce you."

They were no more than ten yards from the bottom of the roll-away staircase, when a cry of excitement sounded from above. Lina's head snapped up in time to see a woman in tight tan breeches and a blue velvet coat much like Yvette's leap from the ship's deck to the top of the stairs. She swung herself onto the handrail and slid to the ground, landing gracefully as a cat.

"Ma petite Redbeard!" The woman raced to Yvette, pulled her into an enthusiastic embrace, and kissed her on both cheeks.

Lina's hands clenched into fists. This was why she wanted that fucking contract torn to shreds. Other people could dash up in the middle of an airfield and put their hands and lips on Yvette—*her* Yvette—and Lina could do nothing but stand and watch in impotent fury.

Fury at others for having what she wanted. Fury at her current self for wanting it so desperately. And fury at her past self for thinking up the contract in the first place.

Yvette and the other captain drew apart, though only far enough to lower Lina's boiling jealousy to a simmer. It still lurked there, ready to flare up again, regardless of how much she despised it.

The two Frenchwomen spoke rapidly in their native

tongue. Lina couldn't pick out a single word until Yvette said, "Mademoiselle Catalina Navarro."

The woman in the blue coat gave Lina a polite nod.

"Lina," Yvette said. "This is Captain Celeste Javet. She has invited us onboard to discuss our interest in hiring her ship."

"A pleasure to meet you, Captain."

Captain Javet smiled. "A pleasure also to me. Sorry my English is—" She waggled a hand back and forth.

"Far better than my French," Lina pointed out.

"I will translate," Yvette declared. "Allons-y. Let's go."

In minutes, all three women were settled in an elegant parlor with coffee and tiny cakes. A crystal chandelier overhead filled the room with warm electric light, highlighting gilt-framed artwork and silver candlesticks. The rug beneath their feet boasted swirling floral patterns as unfaded as if they'd been woven yesterday. Captain Javet wasn't overstating with the designation "de luxe."

Lina sipped from her steaming mug and watched Yvette, trying to follow the conversation based on her gestures and expressions. She didn't translate most of her conversation with Captain Javet, but she did pause now and then to give Lina a brief summary.

"Celeste says her ship can do what we need," Yvette announced. "We are negotiating payment."

"Ask your pal Evan to pay her. He has plenty to spare."

Lina had meant the words as a jest, but Yvette's face lit up. "That's an excellent idea! I think he would be happy to contribute to our efforts. I will telephone him from the airfield office and offer to send a bottle of my best Champagne in thanks."

Yvette turned back to Captain Javet and began to chatter animatedly. Before long, Lina recognized the words, "l'hôtel Waldorf-Astoria." Yvette made a swooping gesture and then a bear growl, her eyes shining as she apparently related the entire tale of their New York adventure.

Lina's heart melted.

I want this woman in my life. I need her in my life. *Now. Forever. I… I love her.*

Of course she did. It was impossible not to adore Yvette. Yvette who befriended millionaires and flew like a bat. Who fought like a hero and kissed like a goddess. Who was strong and fierce but soft and vulnerable. Captain Yvette Séverin wasn't just a pirate, she was the pirate's hidden treasure.

And Lina would walk to the ends of the earth to claim her.

If only she had a map.

<h1 style="text-align:center">28</h1>

"Have fun storming the castle, ladies!"

Zahra's words barely cut through the howl of the wind. Snow swirled through the air, seemingly from all directions at once. Already a thin white film had built up on the deck.

Yvette glanced up to where she knew the castle stood, seeing nothing but blackness. The falling snow and the clouds blotted out the moon and stars, cutting visibility to barely more than the width of the ship.

She stepped cautiously across the slippery planks. This was a good night for stealth, but a dangerous one.

She descended the rope ladder and found her footing on the rocky mountainside before checking the anchors holding the ship in place. The heavy iron spikes were buried deep in the rocks, without the slightest wiggle. Worth the exorbitant price she'd paid. The ship wouldn't be going anywhere, and in case of emergency, Zahra would remain at the helm.

Yvette gave a signal, and the rest of her team climbed down to join her.

Un, deux, trois, quatre, cinq.

All accounted for. No one would be lost in the storm or left behind in the castle under her watch.

"The rocks are sharp," she warned. "But they are not icy

yet, and we only need to climb ten or twelve meters to reach the hidden entrance."

"Ah, yes," Lina murmured. "Only ten meters straight up in the dark in a snowstorm. Easy as pie."

Yvette wasn't sure if Lina had meant her to hear the sarcastic remark, but she couldn't help but respond. "Pie is difficult. That is why I buy pies others bake. This is difficult, too, but not more difficult than you can manage."

"Touché." Lina gave a flirtatious salute and started to climb. "Allons-y!"

Too bad they were climbing a mountain, because Yvette wanted to swoon into Lina's arms. "J'adore quand tu parles français."

"You adore something-or-other French?" Lina grunted and pulled herself higher. "Of course you do."

Angelique scrambled past Yvette, giving her a sly nudge. "Tu adores quelqu'*une* américaine."

Even the biting wind couldn't counter the heat in Yvette's cheeks. She shouldn't have commented on Lina's speaking French. The whole crew knowing about the affair and the whole crew making suggestive remarks about it were two vastly different things. She would need to step carefully.

Thank God she'd rejected Lina's suggestion about changing the contract. Any display of affection in front of the crew would lead to more teasing, and likely to incorrect assumptions. Yvette winced at the thought of the crew pitying her when Lina left. Climbing these rough, cold rocks naked sounded more pleasant.

Yvette climbed slowly, letting the scratch of the jagged terrain on her legs and the chill seeping into her hands distract her from undesired worries. Sometimes life was pain, but she pressed onward. Upward. Her mind settled into focus. She had a job to do.

In no time, she was standing on the narrow, winding path that led from the hidden mountainside exit toward the village below. Somewhere, in the near-vertical rise of stone before her, was the door.

"Security report?"

"This weather will nullify most sensors." Olga moved a hand across the rocks. "Nothing new or unusual here, but opening the door may trigger an alarm. Speed will be important."

The other women nodded their agreement.

"Weapons report?"

"Six Goldschmidt devices each," Kaina replied, patting the bag at her hip.

"Good. When we open the door, you and Esme take the rooms to the right, Olga and Angelique the rooms to the left. Lina and I will head up the secret passage to destroy any equipment in the classrooms. Don't wait for us. If anything goes wrong, we'll escape via the evacuation ship. Any questions?"

Lina lifted one of the apple-sized cylinders from her bag. "I have a question. What is a Goldschmidt device? I was told how to deploy it, but I'm hazy on the details."

Esme waved a hand frantically. "Ooh, ooh, let me!"

Yvette gestured for her to proceed.

"A bloke named Goldschmidt mixed metal powder and metal oxide and—wham!—discovered it burns like the fires o' hell! Started welding railroad tracks with it. Burns so hot and fast it'll destroy what we want without burnin' the whole castle down. The device has a tiny bomb to ignite the reaction, and enough fuel to ruin one of those big dragons."

"Interesting," Lina said, sounding as though she actually meant it. Sounding like a real pirate. Part of the crew. Part of Yvette's life.

We're on a mission. Do the mission. Focus on the mission.

"Olga, please open the door," she instructed.

Olga whipped out a slim tool and slid it into a crack in the rocks that Yvette hadn't noticed until that very second. A muffled *thunk* of shifting metal vibrated from the mountain face. For several seconds, nothing happened. Then, with astonishing smoothness and only a whisper of rolling wheels, the enormous hidden doors swung inward.

Yvette clicked on her torch and led the way.

Lina kept pace with her as they hurried down the long, dark corridor. "What's your excuse for bringing me along this time?"

Yvette caught the subtle uncertainty in the tone, something she might not have noticed if they hadn't been spending so much time together. Did Lina want an excuse? A lie? Because she couldn't cling to the silly "I'm not the spy" idea anymore and they both knew it.

"I wanted to." Maybe Lina would believe the truth this time. "You're smart and competent."

Yvette didn't think Lina realized how much faster and more agile she'd become since joining the crew. She'd scrambled across the theater boxes in New York and climbed the mountainside with ease. Her mind was sharp and she could analyze situations and react quickly. She pushed Yvette to be better. Stronger. Anyone would be proud to have her as a companion.

"And we make a good team."

Believe me. Please believe me. See how good we are together. Don't leave.

A fantasy. Their affair was like the Goldschmidt devices. So hot it could melt anything, but doomed to burn out quickly.

Lina's silence only confirmed this.

"We will come to a staircase at the end of the hall," Yvette said, quashing her heartache with determination. "It spirals up into the castle. Then we'll go through a much smaller hall and up a much smaller staircase that ends at a secret door in a window bench. Once we're in the school we will need absolute silence. Hand gestures only."

"I looked at the map," Lina replied. "I have some idea of

the layout." She ran a finger over the clasps on the pretty corset she wore over her sheer blouse. "I'll stick close to you."

Now there was something hard in her voice. Almost threatening. Yvette wished she could read minds, because she had no time to ask Lina what the problem was. And if she'd caused it.

They jogged up the first staircase, took a few seconds to catch their breath, then proceeded up the final flight at a moderate pace. Time for stealth. Silence. Darkness. And soon… explosions.

Yvette pushed on the mechanism to open the hidden door, then clicked off her torch and tucked it away in her bag. The door opened soundlessly. She reached up and cracked open the lid of the window bench. Dim lights partially illuminated the library beyond. Not even the faintest noise reached her ears. If anyone was lying in wait, they were well hidden. She pushed the bench fully open and hauled herself out.

Lina reached her side a moment later, gently closing the bench behind her. The action came in the nick of time, barely muffling a sharp *bang* from deep below. The first of the Goldschmidt devices.

Yvette motioned for Lina to follow and wove her way around tables and curio cabinets toward the door at the opposite end of the room. The door had been replaced since Yvette had last seen it, and she opened it to the sight of flame-blackened walls devoid of any art or hangings.

She swallowed a laugh. Sabine's duke had caused chaos here not so long ago.

A sound in the distance gave her pause. The creak could be nothing more than the natural settling of an old building. Or a footstep on a loose floorboard.

Yvette waved a hand in a gesture Lina would hopefully interpret as "hurry" and started running toward the classroom halls. This area of the castle had been shut down for the night, without even the dimmest of lamps, and Yvette had to once again turn on her torch.

Lina grabbed the closest doorknob and turned it, holding the door ajar for Yvette to poke the torch inside and take a look. Desks and a blackboard. No science or engineering equipment.

A quick locking of eyes was all they needed to communicate. *Keep going.*

They moved down the hall in perfect synchronization. Open door, peek in. Open door, peek in. Not a sound, not a misstep. No one—not Yvette, Lina, or any outsider—could doubt the truth. They didn't simply make a good team. They made an exceptional team.

The door at the furthest end of the hall finally brought the results they wanted: a room full of drafting tables, blueprints, and tools.

They slipped inside and shut the door. Yvette tore down blueprints from the walls, grabbed others from desks, and shoved them all into the classroom sink. She set a Goldschmidt device in the center of the pile. Not far off, Lina put one of her own devices onto a shelf crammed with tools for building small machines. She held up her box of matches.

Yvette gave a nod, and they lit the fuses at the same time, then scurried away, putting hands over ears.

The *bang* was no worse than a child's firecracker, but still startling in the silence. A moment later, white-hot flames and clouds of sparks erupted from the devices, brilliant balls of destructive beauty, consuming everything in their path. The flares lasted only seconds before dying down into nothing but pools of molten metal in the midst of charred and melted debris.

"Incredible," Lina breathed, her voice thick with awe.

Yvette beamed at her. "Oui." *As incredible as you, my lovely pirate.*

She gestured to two additional places, and they deployed more devices before hurrying out of the room.

An indecipherable shout echoed down the corridor, accompanied by the thuds and stomps of people rushing about. Yvette and Lina raced to the second hall of classrooms, flinging open doors with little concern for stealth. Only one science classroom appeared of possible use in crafting machines, and they stuffed bombs into cabinets of tools and chemicals. As they tore from the room, the devices detonated behind them. They had barely stepped into the hall when a much larger explosion shook the floor beneath them.

Lina yelped.

Yvette cursed. She hadn't considered the inflammability of her targets.

"The classrooms!" someone shouted.

"Up the stairs," Yvette hissed. Unfortunately, the stairs were the same direction as the voices. She drew her knife. "We may have company."

Lina fiddled with one of the clasps on her corset. A sliver of metal popped out the bottom of one busk. Lina yanked on it, releasing a slim blade. The weapon sat comfortably in her hand, like she'd practiced with it. Like she'd been a pirate queen all along.

"Je t—" Yvette cut herself off before she could blurt out the truth. Right now was for showing love, not declaring it. She charged down the hall, her own knife at the ready.

A group of four women came barreling around a corner, but faltered when they spied the gleam of Yvette's weapon. One of them fumbled for a weapon of her own. Yvette plowed into her before she could get hold of it, knocking her hard on her back.

A hand grabbed hold of Yvette's right arm, but she twisted and jabbed her left elbow into her enemy's gut. The woman doubled over and Yvette broke loose.

The two other women had converged on Lina, both now wielding knives of their own. Lina made a wide slash at approximately eye level of her adversaries. The swing didn't reach them, but held their attention enough for Yvette to stab her own blade into the exposed side of one of the women.

As the woman cried out and staggered, Lina dodged, leapt over the enemy lying groaning on the floor, and ran for the stairs. Yvette delivered a final roundhouse kick to the last woman standing, then charged after her fierce, magnificent lover.

More footsteps pounded toward them, along with cries of, "Stop them!"

"No!" boomed the commanding voice of Headmistress von Arx. "*Kill* them."

Yvette yanked one of her remaining Goldschmidt devices from her bag. "Go, go, go!" she shouted to Lina, waving her up the stairs.

Lina didn't hesitate.

Yvette lit the device, dropped it on the bottom step, and flew after Lina, taking the stairs three at a time. They reached the top together as the bomb burst behind them.

Startled enemies screamed in shock and fear, but the quick-burning weapon wouldn't delay them for long. Legs and lungs burning, Yvette raced for the dormitory wing, praying she'd memorized the map correctly. She'd never been a teacher or student, and had only ever visited the public spaces of the castle.

"Brigid!" she shouted. "Hold the ship!"

"Captain!"

Yvette pivoted toward the sound of the voice. "Chantal?"

The twin pirates popped out from around a corner, shepherding half-a-dozen nightgown-clad girls. The students clutched dolls and bags of possessions, looking around with wide eyes. The smallest girl sniffled as she walked, but the others moved calmly, surprised, but not terrified.

"Follow us." Chantal beckoned to Lina and Yvette. "This is the last group. Brigid is helping the others board."

Yvette sprinted to join them, motioning for the twins to hurry. "Bad company coming. Be quick!"

Chantal set the pace, murmuring encouragement to the girls jogging beside her. Her sister took the rear, ensuring none of the students fell behind.

Yvette nudged Clara forward. "Help the students. I'll watch your back."

Clara leapt to obey, taking bags from the girls to leave them free to run. Angry shouts rose behind them. A pistol shot cracked through the air. Several girls screamed.

Lina darted past Yvette and swept the small, crying girl up into her arms. "Hurry! We can make it!"

Yvette paused long enough to throw her final Goldschmidt device in the path of the onrushing enemies, before following her crew and the evacuees to the remains of a large bay window. Brigid stood beside it, helping each student over the shattered panes and onto the gangplank that led to Captain Javet's ship. Snow swirled in the gusting wind, catching on hair and eyelashes and leaving every step damp and slippery. The gangplank swayed and trembled.

Clara and Chantal boosted the girls up and out the window, guiding them across the frigid bridge and into the safety of the ship. Lina scrambled after, the littlest girl still in her arms.

Yvette clapped a hand on Brigid's shoulder, urging her forward. "Well done! Let's fly!"

Another shot rang out, and Yvette ducked instinctively. Bits of stone stung her cheek and arm. Glass crunched beneath her boots.

Brigid scurried up the gangplank, shouting for the ship to take off. Yvette dove after her, clinging to the gangplank rails as it began to pull away from the window. The frozen metal burned her palms and the wet snow began to soak into her clothing. Multiple pairs of hands grabbed her arms, and her crew hauled her the rest of the way to safety. Several more gunshots echoed from inside the castle, but with the howling storm they had little chance of hitting their intended target.

Yvette pushed herself to her feet. Clara and Chantal stood side-by-side, beaming with pride. Nearby, Brigid spoke quietly with a woman who must have been her sister. Dozens of girls and women bunched in groups, some chattering, others comforting one another.

Lina held the hand of the small girl, murmuring soothing words Yvette couldn't make out. She glanced up, met Yvette's eyes, and tapped a finger against her cheek.

Yvette lifted a finger to the same spot on her own face, finding a wet trail of blood from where the shrapnel had struck her. She wiped it away. Just a cut. She tossed a reassuring smile at Lina. "It's nothing."

Lina nodded and returned her attention to the girl.

The airship roared off into the night. Off to starboard, barely visible through the swirl of snow, La Liberté flew alongside. She blinked a signal. Mission accomplished. All crew accounted for.

Yvette's heart soared.

Whatever happened to the Institute, it would no longer be recruiting girls to a criminal enterprise and using them to craft weapons. The biggest operation ever undertaken by the new Captain Rebeard had been a smashing success.

Her eyes drifted back to Lina, who had joined Brigid and the twins in escorting the evacuees down to the luxury cabins for a well-deserved rest.

Her crew had done it. Each and every one of them. She'd never been prouder to be among them.

Yvette bounded toward the group and relieved two women of their heavy bags. Lina cast her a dazzling smile as they all descended the stairs together.

29

YVETTE RUBBED THE STATIONERY between her fingers. As she expected from the finest paper-goods shop in Paris, the quality was excellent. Each sheet had been lightly perfumed with a pleasant rose scent. The variegated pink color was pretty, though faintly reminiscent of watered-down blood. Which was probably the reason the price had been reduced. But also what made it perfect for a sophisticated pirate.

"I'd like all you have of this, including the matching envelopes."

The clerk behind the counter grinned avariciously. "A fine choice, mademoiselle!"

A stroke of luck, honestly, to find all the paper she needed at an excellent price. She had many letters to write. One for each of her crew, one for Captain Javet, one for Brigid's sister Gretchen. Plus Amira, Sabine, Nora… The list seemed to go on forever. So many people to thank. So many who had contributed to her success. She owed them all more than she could repay.

And then there was Lina.

Yvette snagged a small packet of papers with a soft floral trim printed in Lina's favorite shade of blue. "And these."

She would write a beautiful letter confessing all her deepest feelings and present it to Lina with a bouquet and a box of chocolates. Someday. Maybe.

Yvette stole a glance out the window. Lina, Esme, and Clara appeared deep in idle conversation, but they would be alert for any suspicious activity. Vautour could be anywhere. Even if he'd believed Brigid's misleading telegrams, he wouldn't be fooled for long.

Yvette paid for the stationery, then joined the others. "I have what I need. We can continue to Number Seventeen now."

Clara clapped her hands. "I've never been anywhere so scandalous before!"

The girl hadn't stopped smiling since their siege of the castle. Most of the crew, in fact, had been in a perpetual state of good cheer. Their happiness made Yvette want to simultaneously dance and weep. If she could see her friends like this every day, she'd never again regret a single past mistake.

"Madame Séverin provides the most beautiful rooms," Esme replied. "And many beautiful women." She gave Lina a playful nudge and arched her eyebrows. "But I doubt even the prettiest of them can sway you from the captain's side, eh?"

"I have no intention of straying from our stated purpose," Lina replied curtly.

Esme shrugged. "Nor do I. But I'll be enjoying the scenery for sure. I'm blessed to have a matelot who doesn't fear I'll betray her."

Yvette twisted the bag of stationery around in her hand. *Write the letter. Tell her you want what Kaina and Esme have.*

It might be possible. Lina wasn't the sort to betray anyone. But she'd never professed to be the sort to settle down, either. She'd written a contract for a temporary affair, for God's sake.

How could she have known you'd someday want a contract of an entirely different sort?

Yvette fidgeted the rest of the way to the brothel, missing most of what the others said as her brain skipped here and there, writing letters she would never send and imagining futures she would never have. Only once they were safely inside did her body finally relent.

Mimi skipped over shortly after they entered. Today she wore a bright yellow dressing gown loosely tied over nothing at all. She treated the group to her best coquettish smile.

"Welcome, lovely ladies. I am, of course, at your service." Her gaze focused on Yvette. "Your mother wishes to see you in her office."

Yvette reared back in surprise. "My mother?"

"She has information for you. Better than anything I've learned recently, I assume. While you talk, I will show the other ladies our best rooms. The pirate room, of course, and the airship room. Then the beach." Mimi gave Lina a sly grin. "And perhaps the opera."

"You saw the New York newspapers," Yvette guessed.

"Naturellement, ma chérie! Now run along and speak to your mother. I will see to the ladies' every need."

Clara giggled. "My sister is going to be so jealous she wasn't here to see this."

"She might be," Lina replied. "It's a human failing. But she loves you. She'll also be happy to hear you enjoyed your day."

Lina's words circled in Yvette's head as she walked toward her mother's office. She did sometimes envy Esme and Kaina. Or Sabine and her duke. But at the same time, she was overjoyed that they had love and companionship.

It is a "me" problem.

Even more so when she grew jealous over someone flirting with Lina. Lina was a good, caring person. Yvette knew that down to her bones. Lina would never intentionally do her harm. But the feelings still came.

"You look thoughtful, daughter." Yvette's mother waved her into the office. "And a bit vexed, perhaps? I know you rarely confide in me, but I will always listen to whatever you might wish to say."

Yvette closed the door, then took a seat in the chair beside her mother's desk. "I'm bad at trusting people."

The words spilled out. Not because her mother had said anything different than usual, but because for the first time in many years Yvette wanted to trust her. She wanted to trust her crew. Her friends. Especially Lina.

Madame Séverin shook her head sadly. "Your father's doing, no doubt."

Yvette bit her lip. She could speak her mind. Take the plunge. Lady Luck had been with her lately. If there was ever a time, it was now.

"And yours. You…" She had to take a deep breath. "You left me with him."

Her mother's eyes went wide and she let out an audible gasp. A moment later, she sprang from her chair and hurried around the desk to embrace Yvette.

"Oh, my darling. Is this why you stay away? I thought you understood."

Yvette struggled to find words. Her mother was hugging her. She hadn't allowed this in years. Not since she was a child. Today, though, she had no urge to move or pull away. She wanted to be held. Wanted to be loved.

Tears leaked out, along with the question she'd always longed to ask. "Why did you leave me?"

Her mother's grip tightened and she stroked Yvette's hair. "I never left. I was always here, where you could find me."

Yvette shook her head, not understanding. Her mother pressed a kiss to her forehead, then returned to her chair.

"Your father wanted you in his crew. If I tried to take you away or place you with another family, he would have hunted you down, and done harm to those you loved. But you were safe at his side. He wouldn't let his pirates touch you and he wouldn't send you into danger. You were his only blood heir. I wouldn't say he loved you, exactly, but you were a prize. Something he coveted and protected.

"I could have gone away on my own and he would have allowed it. I meant nothing to him. But then I would never have seen you, never known you. So I stayed here. I built a life and fostered connections. I made it my mission to always know what your father was up to, so that whatever happened, I could always find you and vice versa."

The pieces snapped together in Yvette's mind. Why her mother had always seemed to have a network of spies. Why the men and women who worked at Number Seventeen had always made Yvette feel welcome and safe. Why the brothel catered to people of all identities and persuasions. Why her mother had befriended Sabine, at the risk of Redbeard's wrath. This was a Haven. A place Yvette could run to if she needed a roof over her head or an ally on her side.

She dabbed at her eyes with her sleeve. "I'm sorry I didn't understand."

"I'm sorry I wasn't clearer. I tried to do what I thought was best, to let you be safe. And now to be free."

This time Yvette rose and went to hug her mother. The two women embraced in silence for a time, then drew apart through some unspoken agreement.

"You are always, *always* welcome here, my love," her mother said. "And I will always be tracking your exploits. Now, before you tell me all about this new girlfriend of yours, I have information for you about your father's man—the one who calls himself the Vulture."

Yvette leaned over the desk, propping herself up on her elbows. "Tell me."

"The personal airship of Pierre Archambeau departed New York abruptly a number of days ago."

"Terribly shocking."

"Isn't it? Current rumor is that Monsieur Archambeau needed a holiday after the 'hullabaloo at the opera,' as the Americans called it. He is believed to be recuperating at a chalet in the Swiss Alps, after his ship was spotted in the area yesterday."

"Arriving as we were leaving," Yvette mused. "A rendezvous with his ally? Von Arx will be furious and send him to kill us."

Her mother smiled grimly. "I am certain he has wanted you dead since you took up your father's nickname and all his best smuggling routes. But there is more. His other ship—the large ship he uses for piracy—is en route to the hideout in Venice, with most or all of his men."

Yvette's brow furrowed. "Venice? Redbeard had no hideout in that part of Italy."

"It was rarely used. Not since you were small, I believe, but it was never entirely abandoned. It was nothing but a storehouse, and most of the business would have been conducted via water, not the airships you preferred."

A storehouse. Merde. "Big enough to house metal monsters?"

"Oui."

Yvette hopped from her seat. "I need to speak with my crew at once. Thank you for the information."

Madame Séverin nodded. "Be safe. I love you. And bring your girlfriend to meet me when you return. Mimi says you're quite smitten."

Yvette huffed, but she couldn't deny the truth. She impulsively hugged her mother one final time, then scurried from the room. She had letters to write and dragons to slay.

30

LINA RAPPED ON THE DOOR to Yvette's cabin. "All hands on board."

Thud! "Dammit!"

A few seconds and some scrambling noises later, Yvette flung the door open. Her chair had tipped over, and papers lay scattered across the desk and on the floor. "Finally! Let's go."

She scampered up the stairs, calling out for her crew to gather on deck. The pirates came together in a neat circle in the center of the space, leaving a place for Lina beside Yvette.

Lina slipped into the spot as if it were the most natural thing in the world. No one gave her a wink or a sly look. Yvette didn't flush or fidget. Lina's presence at the captain's side was normal, unremarkable. And yet somehow extraordinary.

She belonged here. Truly belonged, in a way she had never quite managed anywhere else. The only way it could feel more right would be if she could give Yvette's hand a squeeze as a sign of her support. But Lina was a woman of her word, and Yvette wanted to keep to their original agreement.

"Thank you, everyone," Yvette began. "I have information to impart, and then we have a decision to make. Together."

Lina's eyebrows lifted. Yvette usually consulted with at least some of her crew over important matters, but now she sounded as though she meant to leave the decision entirely in their hands.

Lina brushed a finger against Yvette's hand, a light enough touch it could be taken as accidental.

Yvette glanced over, and Lina gave her an encouraging smile.

You're doing well. I'm proud of you.

Yvette's lips curved almost imperceptibly, but she launched into her report with enthusiasm, detailing everything she'd learned from Madame Séverin.

"I am certain this hideout contains more of their big dragons," she added, once she'd laid out all the facts. "And I am almost certain Vautour's ship was in Switzerland to transport von Arx and her people to Venice. Together, they will outnumber us at least two-to-one. This may be a trap, to lure us into their territory and destroy us once and for all. It also may be our chance to destroy *them*. I want to go. I want to finish this. But I will not take anyone into danger who does not wish to go. You should each decide for yourself. If we don't have enough to make a crew, we will not go."

Lina took a step forward. "I'm in."

Maybe she wasn't thinking straight. Maybe she had lost all common sense. But someone had to stop these villains, and of everyone in the world, she most trusted Yvette to do it. There wasn't a chance in hell Lina would leave her to do it alone.

Brigid stepped forward. "In."

"In," Chantal and Clara chimed in unison.

Every pirate added her voice to the chorus, firm and clear, no hesitation or uncertainty.

"All of you…" Yvette choked up. She reached for Lina's hand.

Lina jumped at the contact, but quickly entwined their fingers. She squeezed Yvette's hand, her heart pounding in her chest. Partners. No hiding or avoiding.

"You are the finest crew any captain could wish for," Yvette said, her voice thick but adamant. "It is my honor to serve you."

The pirates put fists to their hearts in salute.

"It's our honor to serve *with* you, Captain," Kaina declared. "I'll begin preparations for possible conflict in Venice. The ship and all of us will be ready."

"And I'll take first shift at the helm," Zahra added. "You should have a few hours to rest. You've been busy. Spend some time with your sweetheart."

Yvette turned her head toward Lina, glanced down at their joined hands, then back up until their gazes locked.

"About that contract," Lina murmured.

"We're pirates," Yvette replied. "Rules are more like… guidelines."

Lina laughed and swayed closer. When Yvette didn't pull away, she planted a swift kiss on her lips. "Downstairs?"

"Below. You don't say 'downstairs' on a ship."

"Wherever. Just take me there."

They started for the stairs.

"Captain!" Angelique scurried over and thrust a paper-wrapped parcel at Yvette. "From your favorite shop, as you requested."

Yvette's eyes lit up as she took the package. "Merci!"

"Something exciting?" Lina asked.

"Bonbons!" Yvette bounded down the stairs, half-dragging Lina with her.

"Ah. You do have a sweet tooth. May I sample one?"

Yvette's gaze raked up and down Lina's body, sparking a surge of arousal. "Maybe." She gave Lina an arch grin, then skipped off toward her cabin. She swung the door open, then paused. "Oh, blast. I forgot the mess."

Yvette moved toward the desk and shoved papers into an untidy pile to make room for the package of bonbons. She pulled out her knife to cut the string and started unwrapping.

Lina righted the chair and bent to retrieve the papers that

had fallen to the floor. Most sheets had salutations or partially composed letters scrawled across the top. She gathered them into a tidy bundle and placed it atop the other papers. A single sheet decorated with pastel blue flowers caught her eye, and she tugged it free from the jumble.

"Why is this one different?"

Yvette's hand stilled. She hesitated a moment, then said, "That one will be for you."

Lina scanned the as-yet unaddressed letter. Two short lines in French had been written across the top.

La vie est une fleur,

l'amour en est le miel.

"Life is a flower?"

Yvette beamed. "Très bien!"

"What is miel?" Lina asked, probably mangling the pronunciation.

"Miel means honey."

Lina scanned the words again. "So it's saying that love is the honey—the nectar—of life. What makes it sweet and fragrant, beyond the beauty you see on the surface. That's a lovely sentiment."

"It's the start of a popular poem."

Lina bumped her shoulder against Yvette's. "So you're sending me love poems now?"

"I am writing them." Yvette finished unwrapping her package and plucked a small chocolate from the box. "I do not yet know if I will send them." She bit the chocolate in half. "Mmm. Cherry."

The mingled scent of fruit and liqueur filled the air, and Lina inhaled deeply. "Why would you not send me the love poem?" She leaned in, eager for a taste of chocolate from Yvette's lips. "I assure you, it will be well received."

For a moment, Yvette didn't reply. Her eyes fixed on a point off in the distance, and she absently popped the remaining half bonbon into her mouth. This time the sweet drew no noises of pleasure from her.

"You would like the poem," she said at last, her voice quiet, detached. "But what of my own words?"

All the breath rushed out of Lina's lungs. She cupped Yvette's chin in her hand, tilting her head up to stare into her eyes. Eyes that were stark with vulnerability, and as beautiful as Lina had ever seen.

She brushed her lips over Yvette's, catching a taste of the bonbon she'd eaten. Rich, from the chocolate. Sweet and tart, from the cherry. And with the sharp tingle of alcohol. This was Yvette's taste. Like a summer day with a hint of sin. Crisp, delicious, decadent.

"I adore all things that come from these lips," Lina vowed. "Be they words or kisses. No poem can match the beauty of your true feelings."

Yvette flung her arms around Lina's neck and kissed her so hard she staggered.

Yes, oh, God, yes.

The kiss was powerful, greedy, demanding. With every flick of her tongue, Yvette told Lina what she wanted, how she wanted it. Yvette struggled with uncertainty, and she was naturally impulsive, but when she acted, she gave all of herself. Now, when she asked for all of Lina, there was only one possible answer.

Lina surrendered. She let Yvette sweep her away with the kiss and maneuver her toward the bed, stumbling backward until she bumped into it and fell onto the mattress.

Yvette stepped away. "Take off your clothes," she commanded.

"Bossy today, are we?" Lina smiled so wide she probably looked goofy rather than seductive, but she didn't care. Yvette wanted to send her love poems. Yvette kissed her as if she were staking claim. Nothing else mattered.

Yvette's brows knit together. "Is that good or bad?"

"Everything is good. I like bossy Yvette as much as I like

Yvette who wants me to be the bossy one. Whatever you're feeling today, I'm ready for it."

Yvette folded her arms across her chest. An arch smile played on her lips. "Then why aren't you undressing, wench? Your captain gave you an order."

Lina took the top button of her shirt between two fingers and methodically wriggled it through the buttonhole. "I'm so sorry, Captain," she purred. "Whatever can I do to make it up to you?"

Yvette returned to the table and picked up the box of bonbons. "Hmm." She studied the candies as she turned toward Lina. "Which one should I try next?"

Lina continued to the next button, in the same leisurely manner. "Anything you like, Captain."

Yvette inched closer to the bed, but stayed out of arm's reach. She continued to examine the bonbons.

So this was to be a test of wills. Lina could work with that. She carried on undressing at the same pace. Yvette would crack eventually.

"This one looks delicious." Yvette selected a bonbon and touched it to her lips. Her tongue snaked out to lick the chocolate. "Mmm, yes."

Heat washed over Lina's body. Her fingers twitched, reaching involuntarily for the next button.

Yvette took a tiny bite of the candy and moaned.

"Dammit, you win." Lina undid one final button, then yanked the shirt up and over her head. Her nipples strained against her corset. "Get over here."

Yvette took another bite, making more orgasmic noises. "*I* am the bossy one today. I will come when I am ready." Her eyebrows lifted. "You will come when I say so."

"Madre de Dios," Lina swore breathlessly.

Yvette lost a bit of her swagger. "Too bossy?"

Lina swiftly unclipped her corset busks and tossed the

garment aside. "Don't doubt yourself. I'm dying over here. You made me swear like my grandmother."

"Ah." Yvette finished the bonbon and languidly sucked the remnants from her fingers. "Naughty girl."

Lina shoved her skirt and drawers down together, desperate to get a hand between her legs. "So naughty," she agreed, stroking herself.

Yvette shucked her jacket, boots, and vest, then joined Lina on the bed, bringing the chocolates with her. She tugged on Lina's chemise, and Lina obediently discarded it. Yvette propped herself up on one elbow and raked her molten gaze up and down Lina's naked body.

"Do I make you hot?" she murmured.

"Boiling," Lina sighed.

"Mmm." Yvette selected a bonbon and rolled it between her fingers. "Did you know that the human body is thirty-seven degrees? But chocolate starts to melt between thirty and thirty-two."

She pressed the bonbon against Lina's chest and dragged it down between her breasts, leaving a trail of chocolate. When she stroked her tongue along the same path, Lina moaned.

"Oh, God." She increased the speed of her self-pleasure, rubbing her clit harder, until Yvette stilled her hand.

"Lentement, mon amour. Slowly." Yvette began to draw swirls of chocolate up and around Lina's breasts. "I am not finished with you." She traced the pattern with her tongue, laving each breast, sucking the nipples to aching peaks.

"Wicked pirate," Lina gasped. "So deliciously… diabolical."

Yvette moved down Lina's belly. "Very delicious. And after we are done I will need to take you to the bath and scrub you all over." She licked away another trail of chocolate, then lifted the partially melted bonbon to Lina's lips. "Does this give you pleasure?"

Lina ate the chocolate. "Yes."

"And this?" Yvette pressed a chocolate-coated finger

to Lina's lips, but withdrew it before Lina could suck the delectable digit into her mouth.

"More. Please."

Yvette twisted, lowering her clean left hand to Lina's thigh. "Show me how much I please you. Show me while I am inside you here." She returned the chocolate-covered finger to Lina's lips. "And here." Her left hand eased between Lina's legs.

Lina's eyes fluttered closed. She sucked every morsel of candy from Yvette's finger. Her own fingers moved in relentless circles against her clitoris, building the pressure, nudging her ever closer to the edge.

"Oui, mon amour. Ma belle. Mon trésor."

Lina's breath turned to desperate panting as Yvette's fingers slid inside her, curling and stroking. Perfect Yvette. Brave, beautiful, brilliant Yvette. Yvette who was afraid, but never gave up. Who seized adventure and grew every day into a more powerful, more glorious woman.

"Now, you may come for me," Yvette whispered.

Lina shattered.

Surely the whole world could hear her cry of ecstasy. Let them listen. She wanted them to know the heights of her passion. The depths of her love.

When the spasms relented, her arms dropped limply to her sides and her chest rose and fell in heaving breaths. She opened her eyes to meet Yvette's adoring gaze.

"Now love shakes my soul, as a mountain wind o'erwhelms the oaks," Lina quoted.

Yvette's eyes gleamed a dark, heated blue. "Beautiful."

"It's from Sappho's poems. Words of a woman loving a woman." Lina's heart thudded in her chest, beating out the truth she no longer feared to speak. "As I love you."

31

YVETTE DASHED THE TEARS from her eyes. "Captain Redbeard isn't supposed to cry. How can I be fierce when you make beautiful declarations of love?"

Catalina's dark eyes were so soft and deep, Yvette thought she might fall into her gaze and never emerge again.

An impish smile played across Lina's lips. "You could growl that I'm yours now and you'll gut anyone who tries to take me from you."

Yvette's heart leapt. For an instant, her dream was real. She was sailing the skies, year-after-year, with Lina at her side, surrounded by a crew of friends. For the moment, she would pretend she knew how to get from here to there.

She straddled Lina and gave her a gentle, lingering kiss. "You are mine," she said in her best growling voice. "Don't even think about trying to escape."

When Lina laughed, a surge of pride filled Yvette's chest. It had been scary to step into this role. Even now, the fear of displeasing her partner lingered. She'd always been so certain that if she overstepped, rejection would follow. But she'd done it. And Lina hadn't rejected her.

Lina loved her. Encouraged and accepted her. Not as haughty Redbeard. Not as damaged Yvette who struggled to trust. But as someone who encompassed both those things and more. She could be happy, sad, scared, angry, fierce, or uncertain. And Lina would take her as she was.

"You growl well, my lovely pirate," Lina said. "How may I pleasure you?"

Yvette waved a hand at the bedside table. "There's a toy in the drawer." She flopped onto her back. "You may undress me and use it on me."

"Excellent."

Lina retrieved the clockwork phallus from the drawer and wound it. "How would you like it today?"

"Start slow, then get faster," Yvette instructed.

Lina set the dial to the lowest setting, then clicked the switch to the "on" position. The smooth metal shaft buzzed as it gently vibrated. Lina pressed it between Yvette's legs. Even through her trousers, the slight tingle made her sigh.

"Too slow."

Again Lina's musical laughter echoed through the room. "Aye, Captain." She unfastened Yvette's trousers and tugged them off. The sensible cotton drawers followed.

Yvette's back arched when the vibrator touched her bare flesh. After how aroused she'd become while pleasuring Lina, she wasn't going to last long.

"More."

Lina clicked the dial up one notch.

"Mmm." Yvette's eyes drifted closed. "Yes."

Another notch. The vibration against her clit sent echoing pulses throughout her body. Lina clicked the dial again.

"Inside me," Yvette gasped.

Lina obeyed, beginning with a slow, deep thrust, then picking up the speed with every increase in vibration. Her free hand rubbed Yvette's clitoris, matching the rhythmic movement of the dildo.

Yvette writhed. Her fierce pirate persona was gone, and

now Lina was the one in control. She began begging for release, her words a mumbled mixture of English and French.

"Yes, my lovely," Lina cooed, her voice thick with adoration. "Let yourself go. Take your pleasure."

"You—" Yvette choked out. *You are my pleasure. My lover. My love.*

The orgasm ripped through her, tightening and twisting her body in a glorious spasm that wrung every bit of tension from her muscles. Lina gentled her strokes and turned down the vibration, easing Yvette through the aftershocks before withdrawing completely.

Yvette stared up at the ceiling, breathing deep while the thudding of her heart gradually returned to normal. Lina, flushed and disheveled and beautiful, continued to smile down at her.

That's how she sees me. I am her disheveled beauty.

"Je t'aime," she declared. "I love you. I will finish the letter for you so you may keep it always."

Lina lowered herself to Yvette's side and snuggled close. "I will treasure it," she promised. "Perhaps I'll write you a letter in return."

"I would like that."

She would keep it forever. She wanted to keep Lina forever. But this was entirely new territory, and her body and mind were spent from lovemaking. The future seemed so far away. So nebulous. She could only cling to the here and now and wrap her arms around her love.

"Shall we rest for a while and then go repeat this exercise in your marvelous bathtub?" Lina asked.

"Mmm-hmm," Yvette murmured sleepily.

Lina brushed a stray lock of hair off Yvette's forehead, tucking it behind her ear. "I may not be instrumental to the running of this ship, but I can help her captain arrive in Venice relaxed and clean and prepared for anything."

Yvette's eyes snapped wide open. Venice. Vautour and his

pirates. She'd forgotten they existed in the haze of her love and passion. She mumbled a curse.

"I'm not prepared for everything," she replied. "I'm hardly prepared for anything. I can only guess at what we'll face."

Lina caressed her cheek. "You're a brilliant improviser. You have a loyal, well-trained crew. You have a heart as big and strong as anyone I've ever met."

"You will make me cry again," Yvette accused, blinking away a stray tear.

Lina replied with a brief kiss. "I'm afraid I can't apologize for that. Your tears are beautiful. They come from your love, and it's that capacity for love that makes you truly strong. It's the reason you will prevail."

"Dammit." This time Yvette let the tears fall. Whatever happened in the future, she was lucky to have this woman in her life to care for her and believe in her. "Put on a robe and take me to the bath. It's unfair for only one of us to be…" She wiped her eyes on her sleeve. "Moist."

"But, darling," Lina murmured. "I've been 'moist' since you took your first bite of chocolate." Her voice dropped lower. "I'm still nice and wet for you. Would you like to see?"

"Insatiable wench." Yvette kissed her. "Whatever will I do with you?"

Lina paused, her expression growing serious. "I don't know."

"Neither do I." She shook her head, as if that could shake off her uncertainty. "Let's go take our bath."

The future could sort itself out later.

*L*INA GAZED DOWN at the criss-crossing network of canals and bridges, picking out landmarks she'd only seen before in photographs. Spread out below her lay the Piazza San Marco, its basilica a gleaming meld of the Byzantine and the Gothic. The collapse of the nearby bell tower had made international news a few years prior. A square of scaffolding marked the location where it began to rise once more. Further off, Lina spied the impressive white stone of the Rialto bridge. The Grand Canal flowed beneath, dotted with gondolas carrying lovers and tourists. All around, the domes and bell towers of magnificent old churches reached for the heavens, while their faithful parishioners scuttled through tightly-packed neighborhoods and narrow streets like ants in a hill.

Lina left the bow and jogged up to the bridge, where Yvette piloted the ship with near-impenetrable focus.

A wave of fury swept over her. Yvette would miss the beauty and magic of the city, too busy hunting her enemies. It seemed a foolish thing to dwell on, compared to death and destruction, but the human mind reacted oddly in times of stress. If personal affronts to her sweetheart roused Lina's ire, she would use that to her advantage.

"Once we've defeated these bastards, I'm taking you on a romantic tour of the city," she declared.

Yvette barely flinched. "Pardon?"

"Defeat bastards," Lina repeated. "Then romance."

A slight smile came to Yvette's lips. "Yes. I'm waiting for their trap. They must have seen us." She touched the button for the voice amplifier. "Scouting report?"

The speaker crackled, then Esme's voice rang out. "All clear ahead."

"One ship approaching from the southwest," Angelique's voice followed. "Closing in at a steady rate. Identification in progress."

Lina gripped the control panel. "Do you think it's him? Should we try to outrun him?"

"Yes and no. We will only run if we have no other choice. But we must see his trap first. He may drop another monster from his ship or release one from the warehouse."

"And then we'll need to protect civilians, like in New York." A thought clicked in Lina's mind. One that should have come far sooner. "We need to do it before he can swoop in and disable his own creature, painting himself the hero and placing the blame on you. Us. Maybe even all of our friends." She rocked back on her heels. "He bought those termites from Tagget Industries. If he has more, or has copied the company's mark, the blame could fall on Evan. And he and you are both linked to Nora and Owen and Cassidy Mining. And also to Sabine and the Duke of Hartleigh."

Yvette gave a tiny nod, most of her attention still on her piloting. "Vautour will want revenge on everyone connected to his downfall."

"But it's more than that," Lina explained. "He wants to create a power vacuum by discrediting wealthy and influential people. If he can get popular opinion on his side and get his hands on even a portion of Tagget's manufacturing capabilities and Cassidy's luxene production, he could wreak untold havoc."

"Then I am glad we have destroyed most of his monsters."

"You're taking this very calmly."

One blond eyebrow quirked. "Do you want me to be terrified?"

"I want you to be *alive.*"

The speaker crackled. "Oncoming ship identified," Angelique said. "Warship 'The Scourge.' Outward appearance of a transport ship. Estimate twelve cannon."

"Ready weapons," Yvette commanded. "Maintaining speed and course."

"Twelve cannons?" Lina's pulse began to race. "We have one!"

"Two." Yvette turned the wheel slightly to adjust for the wind. "Kaina has completed the refurbishment on our second gun."

"That's not much—"

An inhuman shriek tore through the air, and Lina whirled around, searching frantically for whatever monster Vautour's ship may have loosed.

A second cry joined the first, then another and another, rising higher, louder, screaming like the harpies of legend. Lina clamped her hands over her ears to muffle the cacophony.

She nearly missed Esme's voice coming over the speaker.

"Multiple hostiles incoming!"

"Defensive positions!" Yvette shouted. "Keep them away from the balloon!"

Lina spun back to face the bow. The attack hadn't come from Vautour's ship. The creatures—at least a half-dozen of them—were rising from the north side of the city, metal wings spread wide.

She pulled a revolver from her belt. The other pirates had given her the gun and some basic safety and firing instructions. Her chances of taking down an enemy hovered somewhere near zero. But she could serve as a distraction and deterrent.

"Shout if you need me!" she called to Yvette, before bounding down the stairs to take up a position along the rail.

The dragons charged the ship, still howling their battle

cries. Bat-like wings stretched at least fifteen feet wide, and smoke puffed from reptilian snouts. Pointed teeth and claws glinted in the sunlight. A rider sat atop each creature, steering it toward the ship.

Lina took aim at the closest dragon and fired. She staggered from the recoil, and the shot went wide.

Another shot rang out a second afterward, and this one didn't miss. The bullet flew straight into the dragon's open mouth, silencing its shrieks. The rider jerked on the reins, and the monster slewed wildly, nearly throwing her off.

"Ausgezeichnet!" Brigid cheered. She aimed and fired off a second shot.

Lina moved around the deck as the dragons swooped and dove, firing her pistol only when they threatened to make contact with the ship. A few of her shots hit the dragons, but failed to destroy anything vital.

The other pirates displayed their skills to the fullest, peppering the creatures' wings and bellies with holes. Occasionally, the women flying them fired back, but it appeared the dragons were difficult to control without two hands to steer them.

Yvette kept La Liberté in constant motion, maneuvering her side-to-side or up-and-down to confuse the attackers. The dragons lashed out with teeth and claws, aiming for the balloon and the rigging, but the gunfire from the pirates forced them to retreat and regroup time after time.

A single dragon soared upward, trying to get atop the ship. Yvette was faster. Unable to rise fast enough, the dragon changed course, darting at La Liberté's side. The pirates took aim, but the dragon veered off before it came within firing range.

Another dragon charged, only to turn away the moment a shot rang out. Stalemate. The enemy couldn't get close enough to do serious damage, and the pirates couldn't hit them from any significant distance.

"Hold your fire," Zahra ordered.

Lina shoved her gun back into the holster and raced to the bridge. Despite Yvette's piloting skills, Vautour's ship—and its twelve cannon—continued to draw closer.

Dammit!

"They're waiting us out! Either we'll run out of ammunition or become cannon fodder!"

Yvette nodded, her jaw tightly set. "Oui," she said after a moment's pause. "We will likely take damage. We must man the cannons and prepare to attack." She flipped the voice amplifier on. "Zahra to the helm. Kaina, prepare wing packs and Goldschmidt devices. Esme and Brigid to the cannons. Everyone else maintain positions."

Lina blinked, trying to piece the orders into a clear picture. "Wait. What are you— Dammit, Yvette are you going to attack the enemy ship by yourself?"

"There are multiple wing packs. You can come with me."

Lina gaped.

"We must nullify either the dragons or the ship," Yvette insisted. "The ship is the easier target. She is not as modern as La Liberté, and I know her weaknesses."

Assuming she could get through a crew of twenty armed men without dying. A tremor rolled through Lina's body. Her chest tightened until she could hardly breathe.

No. I can't lose you. I can't. Not now.

Her gaze dropped to the city streets below. The magic was gone. No beauty. No imaginings of a romantic tour. Without that future, without Yvette, it was only a maze of shadowed lanes and narrow pathways—

Lina flung a hand out and gripped Yvette's arm. "I have a better plan. We abandon ship."

Yvette's eyes went wide with horror. This ship was her life. Her home and her means of survival all in one. Her whole future depended on this ship, and Lina had just threatened it.

"Please." Lina put all the love in her heart into her voice. "Trust me."

Yvette reached for the voice amplifier again. "Abort. All hands to the bridge immediately." She clicked the control off and looked into Lina's eyes. "You explain, I'll look for a place to disembark. Quickly. We have only minutes to spare."

The crew, loyal as ever, raced to gather at the helm. Lina raised a hand to get their attention.

"We're taking this fight to the ground," she announced. "We abandon the ship, let it float away, empty and harmless. One person will remain onboard, out of sight of the enemy, to keep her from crashing or becoming entangled somewhere. We leave a wing pack in case emergency evacuation is needed. The rest of us spread out across the city, separating the dragons and destroying them one-by-one. Once that threat is eliminated, then we can go after Vautour."

Yvette's face lit up. She passed the controls to Zahra and stepped into the circle of pirates. "If you get a chance to disable or kill an enemy rider and capture a dragon, do it. If we get one or two in our hands, we can attack The Scourge. I have a plan." She winked at Lina. "Don't worry, it's like my old plan, but better. Everyone, prepare to disembark. Zahra, you're my most experienced pilot. Can you keep our home safe?"

The first mate didn't turn from the wheel, but her voice rang out clearly. "Aye, Captain!"

"Then let's go! Spread out in pairs. Take down the dragons. Rendezvous in the Piazza San Marco."

"Aye!" the pirates chorused.

Lina grasped Yvette's hand. "You and me."

Yvette gave her a squeeze. "Mais oui! Allons-y!"

33

YVETTE STOOD MOTIONLESS on the cobbled pavement of a small Venice square. She clung to Lina's hand, unable to take her eyes off La Liberté. The ship drifted steadily upward, her escape ladders trailing down like plaited locks of hair. Vautour's warship hovered just out of attack range, watching.

The screech of a dragon jolted her awareness back to her body. Time to run. She had to trust Zahra and trust in Lina's plan. She had to do her part.

The other pirates had already scattered, luring a few of the creatures after them. Lina and Yvette had lingered. If this plan was going to work, they had to be certain the enemy had spotted them.

The dragon cried again, swooping down, its claws extended.

"Drago!" a man screamed, pointing upward with one hand while he shielded his head with the other.

"That's our signal!" Lina tugged on Yvette's hand, propelling her into motion.

Yvette took a quick glance up. Three dragons incoming. Good.

They raced southeast, toward the Rialto Bridge, dodging terrified Venetians and stupefied tourists. Even in the chaotic crowd, Yvette's red velvet coat stood out. People leapt out of her way, clearing her path and leaving her enemies a sightline.

"This way, little monsters," she crooned. "Come get me."

Lina's grip on Yvette's hand tightened and she ran faster. "I'm not sure I like this addendum to my plan!"

"I trust you, you trust me. Take the middle path." She pointed at the Rialto's wide, shop-lined central corridor. On this sunny afternoon, all the shops had their awnings extended, providing plenty of cover from any aerial pursuer.

Even after they were out of sight, Yvette continued to run. Pulling Lina with her, she charged up the stepped path, shoving aside any pedestrians or merchandise that impeded her path.

"To the center of the bridge," she commanded. "They need to slow down to watch for us coming out the other side." She released Lina's hand and drew one of her flintlocks. "The central archway is open to both sides. We pop out and take them by surprise."

It was a gamble, but not a terribly risky one. If she was right, and her enemy assumed she would cross the bridge slowly to conserve energy, they wouldn't expect any attack so soon. If she was wrong, all she needed to do was duck back beneath the central arch.

Lina kept close to Yvette's side, whether she agreed with the plan or not. Apparently this was how having a partner worked. You listened to them and they listened to you. You didn't always agree, but when the other person had a good idea or the right experience, you let them take the lead and asked what you could do to help.

"Strange." She let out a little laugh. "But I like it."

"What?"

"Never mind. Almost there." She slowed her pace by half, elbowed her way past a leering, intoxicated man, and turned sharply to the left.

Lina's hand touched her back. "Together."

Yvette nodded and lifted her pistol, and they jogged out into the sunshine.

The dragons were no longer screeching, and she had to squint to search for them in the sky overhead.

"There!" Lina pointed.

Yvette followed the path of Lina's extended arm in time to see a dragon gliding out from above the bridge. In a few seconds, the rider would have the correct angle to spot them.

And Yvette would have a perfect shot. She took aim.

The sounds of people screaming—either because of the dragon or the pirate with a gun—registered only as vague background noise. Her body stilled, only her eyes and hands moving with the target.

Un. Deux.

The gun barked and the woman on the dragon cried out in pain. It wasn't a fatal hit, but it threw her off balance. She flailed for a grip on the creature, but the smooth metal of the body offered no handholds, and she slipped from its back. The splash of her hitting the water below swallowed up her scream.

Without a rider, the dragon lurched into a tumbling downward spiral. It plowed head-first into the canal, spraying water as high as the top of the bridge. The wake from the impact tossed gondolas and soaked the feet of anyone standing near the bank.

"Nice shot," Lina said.

Yvette holstered the gun and took her lover's hand again. They slipped under cover without another look back. Someone would have to deal with the panicked people and the mess in the canal, but she wasn't sticking around for any of that. Two more dragons needed destroying. And, frankly, none of this was her fault.

They hurried on down the far side of the bridge—though at a pace more conducive to breathing. The sparkle of glass and bright colors of feathered Carnevale masks in shop windows made Yvette's head turn a time or two. Or a dozen.

"I want to shop here when it's time for romance. Ooh, hats!" She twisted for a better look at the tall rack hung with a dazzling array of headgear. Among the flowers and feathers sat a tidy leather tricorn much like the one she'd lost in the Paris sewers. They were definitely coming back here.

An explosion sounded in the distance. Another dragon down. Maybe she'd bring the entire crew shopping when this was over.

Yvette and Lina paused at the end of the bridge to prepare for another sprint. Yvette stretched her legs, then checked her weapons. "Are you ready?"

"I am," Lina answered. "But I hope you know where you're going, because I don't. I've never been to Venice before."

"Neither have I, but I have an excellent sense of direction and I have studied the map. Allons-y." She took a fortifying breath and stepped out into the open.

The enemies spotted them almost immediately and steered their dragons into diving attacks. Yvette and Lina ran down the street, then darted right onto a much narrower path just in time to avoid a swiping claw.

"'Tain!" Yvette cursed. "These two are good." The dragons came into view again, tracking them from the rooftops. "We will need to be fast."

"I'll keep up," Lina promised.

I trust you. You trust me. No woman left behind.

They could do this.

Yvette led the way into a dizzying series of twists and turns, reciting approximate directions in her head to keep herself oriented. East. South. West. South. East. She ran until her legs burned and sweat poured down her back—over small bridges, through church squares, and into dark alleys.

Above, the dragons screamed and swooped and screamed some more. One tore a chimney from a roof, sending bricks and mortar flying. Yvette threw up her arms to shield herself, but didn't break her stride.

"Nearly to San Marco! There will be porticos we can shelter beneath."

Lina, breathing heavily, bumped her arm in acknowledgement.

One quick zig-zag later, they staggered across a small bridge into a covered lane. Light spilled from the piazza beyond, pooling on the stone walkway. They sagged against the walls, chests heaving, and peered through the portico arch into the square.

"Now what?" Lina panted.

"I don't know." Yvette took a moment to catch her breath, then walked to the edge of the portico and searched the sky for the dragons. The metal creatures circled silently, like raptors hunting mice in a field.

Lina's hand settled on Yvette's back. "We can either turn around, or we can walk along this colonnade to a different exit. At the speed these two can fly, we'll never make it across the square." Her head turned toward the cathedral. "We could probably get to the church. Go inside and pray for a better plan. Just don't trip over a pigeon. Why is this place so full of them?"

Yvette's gaze swung to the largest cluster of birds. The pigeons strutted boldly across the pavement, announcing to all visitors that this was their square and unless you had food you should move along.

A grin crept over her face. "Because Lady Luck loves me." She spun to face Lina. "I'm going to walk out there and lure the dragons down. On my signal, run out and startle as many pigeons as possible. Fill the air with them."

Before Lina could respond, Yvette kissed her hard on the mouth. Then she pivoted on the balls of her feet, puffed up her chest like the pigeons, and strode out into the square, the tails of her red coat fanning out behind her.

34

"IF YOU DIE I'm going to kill you," Lina shouted, her fists clenching at her sides. She'd known from the first that this was a dangerous mission. But no amount of prior knowledge could prepare one for the sight of one's beloved walking into the line of fire.

"I love you too, mon coeur!" Yvette called back. She ambled into a cluster of pigeons, who seemed to accept her as one of their own.

She *was* bold and liked to preen, Lina supposed. And foolish. So impulsively, bravely foolish.

Why was love like this? Lina might once have said she was better off without an emotion so irrational it made you want to strangle someone and hold them forever at the same time. Now… Well, now she simply accepted the inevitable and braced herself to run.

The dragons circled lower, but didn't dive, the riders too savvy to jump into a possible trap. Yvette continued to walk casually through the square. The pigeons followed. More birds hopped and fluttered to trail after her.

Lina's nose wrinkled. What was she, the damned Pied Piper of pigeons?

Yvette cooed something in French. A trickle of crumbs fell

from her hand, and a dozen birds leapt to peck at it. She was feeding them. She looked up at the dragons and called to them in the same melodious voice.

The dragon riders flew close together, came to some kind of agreement, then separated. They made a final circle of the square, then one dragon dove sharply, aiming straight for Yvette.

Lina's heart pounded. Her muscles tightened to the point of pain. The signal! Where was the damned signal?

Time turned nebulous. The dragon sliced through the air, nearer and nearer.

A gunshot cracked, and Lina jerked, suddenly aware of the revolver in her hand. As usual, she'd missed, but the shot had come close enough to make the pilot veer away from Yvette.

The second dragon dove.

"Now!" Yvette shouted. She flung herself into a wild dance, waving and stomping to startle the pigeons.

Lina ran into the square, shouting nonsense, barreling through clusters of birds.

Time continued to stutter. Clouds of birds rose into the air. People screamed. One of the dragons roared. From somewhere above came the high-pitched crunch of twisting metal. And through it all, the pirate in the red coat spun, a blur of velvet and loose blond hair and the joyous cries of, "Fly, my pretties! Vole, vole!"

Lina reached Yvette's side, and the world shifted back to normal speed. The flying pigeons glided toward the ground, and beyond them a dragon tumbled, one of its wings bent at a strange angle. It plowed into the scaffolding of the under-construction tower. A chunk of the wall collapsed.

Yvette shrugged. "At least it wasn't finished." In the same breath, she drew her second flintlock and fired.

Lina blinked.

The second dragon smacked the pavement and slid to an

inelegant halt. Its bloodied rider fell from its back and lay unmoving.

Yvette ran to the dragon and stopped beside her vanquished enemy. "Ah, Headmistress von Arx. I'm afraid that wound may be fatal." She shrugged and clambered up onto the back of the mechanical beast.

Lina avoided looking directly at the fallen rider. She couldn't say she would mourn the woman, but she didn't want to look at her dead body, either.

She put a hand on the reins that dangled from the dragon's neck. "It almost looks like a horse. The way you ride it, I mean. Those look like pressure sensors, there by your knees."

Yvette glanced down. Her brow furrowed.

"Do you know how to ride a horse?" Lina asked.

"Non."

"Then move back." She shooed Yvette from the seat. "I'll fly, you do… whatever it is you plan to do."

Yvette's smile was feral. "Destroy the vulture." She slid back to make room for Lina.

Lina slung a leg over the dragon's back and settled herself into the saddle-like seat. She took a few moments to study the controls. One altimeter and three unmarked switches. Great.

A shrill whistle blew, followed by a series of angry words in Italian. The only one Lina could pick out was, "Pirata!"

"Time to go!" Yvette reached a hand past Lina and flipped one of the switches. The dragon shrieked. She quickly shut it off and flipped another switch. The creature's wings began to flap.

Lina nudged the dragon as if it were a horse, and it lurched forward.

One damaged leg. Dent in the side where the other dragon struck it. Here goes nothing.

She squeezed her legs tighter. "Giddyup!"

The dragon took two more wobbly steps, then launched itself into the air.

They rose in a wobbling spiral, listing perilously from side-to-side as Lina learned the feel of the dragon beneath her. Sweat slicked her hands where she grasped the reins. Her stomach churned. Yvette's arms clamped around her waist. If they fell, they fell together.

A gust of wind shook them so hard they bounced in the saddle. Yvette yelped.

Lina grunted and gritted her teeth as she steadied the dragon. "This is why horses only move in two dimensions," she grumbled.

"They can jump," Yvette pointed out, her voice surprisingly calm for someone currently clinging to Lina for dear life.

Out of the corner of her eye, Lina spotted the glint of another dragon. She glanced over to see it careening—riderless—into the city below.

Not this high.

Her spine straightened. This was no time for fatalism. She was a pirate, and pirates fought to the bitter end.

"Seems I'm a storybook hero after all."

Yvette squeezed her. "Yes. We will ride into battle and then you can carry me away to your castle."

Absolutely. Lina would happily play the knight in shining armor, now that she'd found the right princess. "Where's the enemy ship?"

"Behind us," Yvette said. "Hovering over the water. Stalking La Liberté. That scum wants to take her."

Lina urged the dragon into a gently-banked turn—her best so far. "He can't have her. What do you need me to do?"

"Get as high as possible. And hope I am good at throwing."

Lina steered the dragon upward, her confidence rising with the altitude. Unlike a horse, the dragon had no mind of its own, making its motions entirely predictable once you learned them.

Even having seen the dragons in flight, Lina was surprised at their speed. It felt like mere moments before they drew close enough to pick out individual pirates among Vautour's crew. The men paid them no heed as they flew closer.

"They must think we're with the dragon riders," Lina guessed.

"Mmm," Yvette agreed. "They are not the sort of men who pay attention to the women helping them. And that is why they will fail. A little higher, if you can. Above the balloon."

Lina nodded and pressed her mount onward. She was only a few yards shy of her desired altitude when a cry of alarm rose from the ship's deck.

Yvette chucked something small and brown at the ship. It bounced off the balloon and tumbled toward the ground. "Close enough," she declared.

"What was that?"

"My last chocolate biscuit." Yvette sighed. "The pigeons ate the others."

Lina's heart stuttered with affection for her eccentric pirate captain. "I am kissing you as soon as humanly possible." A gunshot rang out, and she winced. "After the battle!" She and Yvette were difficult targets from below, but already the dragon was battered and pockmarked with holes. She couldn't begin to guess how much more it could withstand.

Yvette shuffled around behind her. The smell of burning phosphorus hit Lina's nose the moment Yvette began to count.

"Un, deux, trois!"

A small metal cylinder flew through the air, exploding into an inferno of sparks and flames above the ship's balloon. A Goldschmidt device!

Yvette hurled a second bomb right as the molten metal from the first reaction splattered across the balloon, searing holes through the skin.

"Go, go!" Yvette cried.

Lina banked away from the ship. The explosion of the second Goldschmidt device was lost in the *whoosh* of igniting gas. Lina yelped and squeezed her knees, propelling the dragon faster. Heat and smoke roiled through the air. By the time she dared glance back, the entire ship was engulfed in flames, chunks of charred and twisted debris already tumbling to the water below.

"Madre de Dios," she gasped. "That thing was full of hydrogen!"

"Oui," Yvette confirmed. "When *I* chose which of my father's ships to make my own, I chose the most modern, safest ship. Vautour was a fool." She sniffed. "He chose a hydrogen ship, because it can go faster and carry more cargo. He could make more money in fewer trips. His greed is his downfall."

Lina's gaze snagged on the flaming wreckage plummeting into the sea. "In an oddly literal manner. Back to San Marco?"

"Oui. We will wait for the others, then signal to Zahra to pick us up."

Lina guided the dragon into a wide descending circle. After a few minutes she managed a halting landing that nearly unseated her.

"I'll have to work on that part." She let Yvette slide off before dismounting herself. "I think we should keep him." She patted the dragon's head. "We can call him Marco."

"As you wish, my knight."

Lina slid an arm around her love. "Can you believe I had convinced myself such fantasies were childish? Years ago, my lover, Emily—the girl next door—became engaged to a man her parents chose." The story she'd hidden out of shame spilled out, now nothing more than a piece of the woman she'd become. "I packed my bags, saddled my horse, and climbed into her bedroom to rescue her. Only to leave in heartbreak and scandal when she grew angry and shouted that she didn't want to be rescued. I thought I was so foolish."

Yvette made a noise of disgust. "*She* was foolish. I would be rescued by you any day."

"Emily had different priorities," Lina explained. "She wasn't right for me. But the incident did lead me to study the human mind. I wanted to know how two people so much the same could also be so different. And ultimately, that led me to you, the greatest adventure of my life."

Yvette turned an adorable shade of pink. "You…" She broke off with a cry of dismay. "Those stupid pigeons!" She lifted one tail of her coat. An ugly white splotch stood out against the red velvet. "Look what they've done! And after I fed them my biscuits!"

Lina nodded in sympathy. "To be fair, you also did scare them."

"Hmph. That is no excuse for befouling a fine fabric. Where is my ship? This needs to be washed at once!"

"I wouldn't bother," purred a low, sinister voice.

Lina and Yvette both spun around. Vautour strode toward them, a sword in one hand and a dagger in the other. Pigeons darted out of his path.

Yvette drew her knife.

The assassin laughed. "That coat will be stained with your blood soon enough."

35

YVETTE SCOWLED AT VAUTOUR. "Why can't you just die?" She took a quick glance around, but no one was looking in their direction. Official-looking people were fussing over the damaged tower and the dead bodies. Everyone else was gone, unless they were hiding in the shadows beneath the porticos or sheltering inside the church.

Lina took hold of her arm and pulled her behind the dragon.

Vautour snarled and sheathed his weapons. "Very well." He drew a gun. "I didn't wish to make noise, but—" He staggered. "G-ga—" He fell face-down on the pavement. Five knives of various sizes jutted from his back.

Yvette's pirates swarmed from the portico.

"Should've known better than to attack our captain." Esme plucked out one of the knives and cleaned it on the dead man's clothes.

"Thank you," Yvette replied.

Esme shrugged. "Only fair, after you destroyed his ship."

Yvette took Lina's hand and pressed a kiss to her knuckles. "I couldn't have done it without my dearest Catalina." She placed her other hand on the dragon. "And Marco. We may have to make room for him on the ship."

"I can patch him up so he is good as new," Brigid said.

Chantal waved a hand. "Ooh, maybe we can rig a tether so he glides behind us. He would scare people away."

Kaina cleared her throat. "I will be the practical pirate today, and suggest we move away from the dead man and signal to Zahra."

"I agree one hundred percent," Lina said. "Venice is an interesting city, but right now I can't wait to get home."

Yvette flinched. Home. This portion of her life was over. Mission objectives accomplished, enemies vanquished. It was time to return to normal life.

Except that she wasn't the same Yvette she'd been then, and she didn't know what "normal" meant for her anymore. She knew what it meant for Lina, though.

"We will fly to Savannah as soon as we are able," she said, in a voice of calm resignation. Not her usual captain's voice, but maybe that of a captain going down with the ship. "Your help and presence have been… invaluable."

"What?" Lina's head tilted to the side as she regarded Yvette with a frown of bafflement. "What do you— Oh! No, I meant home to our ship."

"Our ship," Yvette echoed.

Lina put her hands on her hips. "Did you not hear the part where I said you are my greatest adventure?"

The pirates clustered around Lina and Yvette, eager grins on all their faces.

"Kiss her, Captain!" Clara urged.

"Our. Ship." The words drummed in Yvette's head. "But you… This was temporary. You meant to leave." The very idea sounded ludicrous beside the effervescent fountain of hope rising inside her. "Or have you reconsidered?"

Lina took both Yvette's hands in hers and looked her straight in the eye. "You kidnapped me, remember? What kind of pirate lets her captive go?"

"A pirate who wants her lady to have a choice in the matter."

"Well, I had a choice. And I chose you."

A smile spread across Yvette's face until she was grinning so hard it almost hurt. "Are you certain? I am difficult. I am impulsive and brash and often uncertain. Most days I am a hot mess."

"Well, I can be self-important and surly, and you don't seem to mind that."

Clara let out a sigh. "Are they ever going to kiss?" she whispered to her twin.

Lina laughed. "And how could I give up a life like this?" She waved a hand to indicate the pirates, the dragon, and the mess they'd left in their wake. "To go back to a life that was stale and unfulfilling? You, Captain Yvette Séverin, have given me the opportunity to see the world in the company of good and loyal women."

"We're also thieves and smugglers," Brigid pointed out.

Lina shrugged. "I will never be bored." She gave Yvette's fingers a squeeze. "And I will have the woman I love always at my side."

"Or at your back." Yvette winked. "Or on top of you." She leaned in and gave Lina a brief, tender kiss.

Clara clapped and cheered.

"More later," Yvette murmured. She drew back, then said aloud, "Let's get to the ship. I have an important question to ask crewwoman Catalina in private, and hopefully a contract to draft. Later we will all go shopping and have gondola rides." She tilted her chin up and straightened her lapels. "We are sophisticated, romantic pirates, and we will celebrate in style."

Kaina lit the signal flare, and Lina and Yvette climbed onto Marco the dragon.

"Shopping and romance, eh, love?" Lina wriggled in her seat, sparking a shiver of desire in Yvette's belly. "Are you by any chance planning a fancy matelotage ceremony?"

"Oui. If you will marry me?" The question sent spikes of

anxiety through every cell in her body, but Captain Redbeard had learned to face her fears. The only way to win was to try.

Lina turned to peck Yvette on the cheek, then started up the dragon.

"Aye, Captain. I will."

Yvette's heart soared, higher than any dragon or airship could ever match.

LINA DIDN'T EVEN TRY to hold back her tears as she gazed into Yvette's misty blue eyes. Today was a day of joy and she wanted the world to see.

"You are so beautiful," she whispered.

Yvette ran a hand down her splendid white tailcoat and fiddled with one of the gold buttons. She was a diamond shining in the sun, from her highly polished boots to her pristinely white coat and trousers, to her gold waistcoat. Lina couldn't have imagined a more magnificent pirate bride.

"So are you. Twirl for me."

Lina spun, causing the sleek satin of her simple wedding gown to fan out around her ankles. Yvette grinned at the flash of silver-embroidered stocking.

"It will be fun to undress you today."

Nora, the "minister" for this ceremony, coughed. "The vows, ladies."

Yvette waved a hand. "Oui, oui. Catalina, I promise to love you and take care of you and share all my worldly goods with you. In the event that you are maimed or lose a limb, I will see that you are taken to Dr. Nora for a biomechanical replacement. And I will even sometimes share my bonbons with you."

Lina's laugh came out almost as a snort and she clapped a hand to her mouth. "My darling Yvette," she finally said in a half-choked voice. "I promise to love you and share my worldly goods with you. I vow that I will attempt to keep you from getting into too much trouble while never stifling your spirit." She glanced at the gathered audience. "Please pray for me."

When the laughter died down, she continued. "I promise to buy you bonbons and share bubble baths, and live happily ever after by your side."

"I now pronounce you Captain and Mate!" Nora declared.

The crowd clapped as Lina and Yvette kissed. Lina lingered for a moment against Yvette's lips, savoring the sensation of unbounded happiness.

A boom so loud it shook the ship startled her out of her trance.

"Fire two!" Esme called.

Another cannon went off.

"Fire three!"

And another. The pirates cheered.

"When did we get a third cannon?" Lina wondered.

Yvette bounced and kissed her cheek. "Happy Matelotage, mon amour!"

"You bought me a cannon?"

"I bought *us* a cannon. For protection. I thought you would like that."

Lina laughed and hugged her wife. Wife. What a lovely word. "I do like it. Now, wife, shall we dance or have cake first?"

"Cake, of course! And Champagne." Yvette gave Lina a little nudge with her elbow. "Come along, wife."

The cake was delicious, the Champagne a perfect balance between sweet and dry, and the dancing gloriously wild and free. Only after they'd completely worn themselves out with merriment did Lina and Yvette step aside for a quiet moment at the bow of the ship.

"Did you have a plan for our honeymoon?" Lina curled an arm around Yvette. "I'm happy to go anywhere, honestly."

Yvette let her head fall onto Lina's shoulder. "I thought so, or you would have said something. What do you think of the rainforest?"

"The rainforest?"

"It sounds exciting, and I have never explored South America. Of course, first we need to sell all the extra Champagne in the hold. Funny how we brought so much more than we needed for the wedding. Then we will stop in Cuba…"

Lina turned Yvette so they were eye-to-eye. "What's in Cuba?"

"Cigars. Many people will want them with the Redbeard discount."

Lina leaned in until her forehead pressed against Yvette's. "I should have known."

Yvette rubbed their noses together. "I am a smuggler, ma chérie."

"Mmm?" Lina pulled her in for a kiss. "What's that, love? A snuggler? I'll snuggle with you any day."

Yvette wound her arms around Lina's neck, and for the next few minutes, they didn't speak.

"You know what I said," Yvette murmured when they came up for air.

Lina held her close, breathing in her perfume and admiring the flush on her cheeks. "I suppose I'll smuggle with you any day too."

Yvette beamed. "I am the luckiest pirate in the world."

Lina didn't believe in luck. Life was random, and most people ended up with some good things and some bad. But she did believe in happiness and in love. And right now, she had so much of both she thought her heart might burst.

"That makes two of us, my dearest, darling captain." She gave Yvette a playful swat on the bum. "Shall we go below and begin our honeymoon?"

Yvette arched her eyebrows in a perfect piratical grin. "Absolutement! A captain always goes down with her ship."

The End

About the Author

Award-winning author Catherine Stein believes that everyone deserves love and that Happily Ever After has the power to help, to heal, and to comfort. She writes sassy, sexy romance set during the Victorian and Edwardian eras. Her stories are full of action, adventure, magic, and fantastic technologies.

Catherine lives in Michigan with her husband and three rambunctious kids. She loves steampunk and Oxford commas, and can often be found dressed in Renaissance festival clothing, drinking copious amounts of tea.

Visit Catherine online at
www.catsteinbooks.com
and join her VIP mailing list for a free short story.

Follow her on Twitter @catsteinbooks,
or like her page on Facebook @catsteinbooks.

Also by CATHERINE STEIN

Potions and Passions

The Earl on the Train - Book 0.5

How to Seduce a Spy - Book 1

Mishaps & Mistletoe -
A Holiday Novella -Book 1.5

Not a Mourning Person - Book 2

Once a Rake, Always a Rogue - Book 3

Love at Second Sight - Book 4

Sass and Steam

Love is in the Airship - Book 0.5

A Shot to the Heart - Book 0.75

Eden's Voice - Book 1

What Are You Doing New Year's Eve? -
A Holiday Novella - Book 1.5

Priceless - Book 2

Sass and Steam (cont.)

Dead Dukes Tell No Tales - Book 3

Beyond Repair - Book 4

Arcane Tales

The Scoundrel's New Con - Book 1

The Spinster's Swindle - Book 2

Mad Scientists Society

The Courtesan and Mr. Hyde - Book 1

Other Books

Mating Habits - Book 1

Idle Nature - Book 2

My Heiress, 'Tis of Thee

Available at your favorite online retailer.
www.catsteinbooks.com

Thank you so much for reading.
If you enjoyed the book and are so inclined, I would love for you to leave a review. Happy readers make an author's day!

I love hearing from readers,
so feel free to contact me on social media, or email:

catherine@catsteinbooks.com